99
1940

D1545679

PAINTED
COMANCHE
TREE

PAINTED
COMANCHE
TREE

•

KENT CONWELL

AVALON BOOKS
THOMAS BOUREGY AND COMPANY, INC.
401 LAFAYETTE STREET
NEW YORK, NEW YORK 10003

PRINTED IN THE UNITED STATES OF AMERICA
ON ACID-FREE PAPER
BY HADDON CRAFTSMEN, BLOOMSBURG, PENNSYLVANIA

To Rogayle, Lela, Jessica, Lauren—a wonderful critique group. And to Gayle, my wife, who tolerates the crazy life of a writer.

Chapter One

My Pa died when I was ten. After that, I knocked about the West from Santa Fe to San Antone, from Denver to Dallas, from Taos to Tombstone, doing everything from swamping saloons to sawyering, from chopping cotton to coopering until I reached man size. I was always looking for a place where I could settle in, where I fit. A home.

With no luck.

Every venture I tried blew up in my face. Every time I thought I saw light at the end of the tunnel, the beam turned out to be the headlamp of a fifty-seven-foot Washington 4-4-0 locomotive. But let some other jasper take the same gamble, nine times out of ten, the scheme blossomed into a moneymaking proposition.

So, I sure wasn't expecting any miracles when I found myself in the middle of a snowstorm with a white-haired Oriental riding behind me on the rump of my roan pony, Ned.

The Oriental, who I called Shoelink because I couldn't pronounce his name, was healing a broken leg, and I was recovering from a rattlesnake bite, another sample of my luck. Reckon I'm the only hombre in the West who got himself bit by a hibernating rattler.

Anyway, there I was, smack-dab in the middle of a blue norther that was howling across the Chihuahuan Desert like a pack of wolves, driving the cold deep into my bones. I

1

huddled down into my mackinaw, trying to pull my head inside. Snowflakes stung my cheek, worked down my up-turned collar, and chilled my neck.

Suddenly, through the gusting snow, a crooked post with a cockeyed sign appeared in front of me.

HANKERING-5 MI

We reached Hankering about midafternoon. The snow had stopped, but several inches covered the ground. I tied Ned up in front of the Hankering Saloon and brushed the snow from my mackinaw as I stomped inside the saloon, favoring my leg. The little Chinese hombre limped after me.

The bar was a rough plank stretched between two oaken barrels. A kerosene lantern hung from the ceiling over each end of the bar.

Four more lanterns dangled from the ceiling joists, one over each table in the room. A rock fireplace filled the far wall. A blazing fire in the hearth was a welcome relief from the cold. Half a dozen cowpokes watched us limp across the room and stop in front of the fire, warming our frozen bodies.

The bartender pushed through the curtains behind the bar.

I nodded and ambled over to the plank. "Howdy."

"Howdy." He frowned at Shoelink.

"Two whiskeys. My innards are colder'n a lake of ice."

"I'll give you a shot, but I don't serve no China Boys, not even old man China Boys," he growled, glaring at Shoelink. "All I serve here is 'Mericans."

His words slapped me across the face. Slowly, I unbut-toned my mackinaw, revealing the hogleg on my hip. "Mister, I got myself snakebit a while back, up in the

Catalinas by Tucson. And for your information, this little China Boy's handle is Shoelink, and he's the one who nursed me through a plug-ugly time. Now, I'd be mighty put out if someone was to refuse me the right to have a sociable drink with the jasper who saved my life.''

The only sound in the saloon was the fire crackling in the hearth.

"Well, stranger," said a garrulous voice near the fire. "You might as well get *put out* because I'm saying the same thing. We don't serve no foreign squint-eyes here." An hombre with shoulders wider than an axe handle rose to his feet. His bulk almost blocked off the fire in the hearth. "We don't want none of them John Chinaman people around here."

"Oh?" I eyed the big man. My cheeks burned. "And who might you be?"

He jutted out a grizzled jaw spiked with three days of beard black as night. "Ain't no *might be* about it. I'm Mike Blake. Don't you forget."

A wizened old man nodded at the large cowpoke standing by his table. "Aye. The lad speaks true, me Boy. This land here be hard and filled with danger. We fit for it, fit hard. We don't want the likes of foreign yummies come in to live on what we 'ave done."

A grin leaped to my face. "You're from the old country, I see. You miss it?"

His wrinkled face broke into a wreath of smiles. "Aye. Faith and begorra, the times I dream of its green hills and shining streams."

I looked back to the wide-shouldered cowpoke glaring down at me. "You know, Mr. Blake," I said with a taunting sneer, "Last I knew, Ireland was on the other side of the ocean. Now, how do you reckon it came to be part of the United States? Like you boys here say, 'Mericans. Why don't you explain that to me, Mr. Blake?''

The old Irish man frowned, puzzled at my question, but Mike Blake understood. With a roar, he lunged at me.

Before I could move, a tiny shadow darted in front of me, grabbed Blake by the arm and vest, twisted, and sent the big man slamming to the floor on his back. The whole building shuddered at the impact.

Shoelink stepped back quickly, folded his hands over his waist and waited, his tiny pillbox hat on the back of his head and his snow-white pigtail hanging down his back. Blake lay motionless, then slowly stirred. He sat up, shook his head, and looked around, finally fixing his eyes on the small Oriental.

Blake shook his head and lumbered to his feet, instantly throwing himself at Shoelink, who, at the last minute, deftly sidestepped, allowing the locomotive of a man to roar past. Blake jerked around.

When he did, Shoelink leaped into the air and smashed his foot into Blake's throat. The giant gasped and clutched his throat. His eyes bulged and he sagged to the floor.

The only sound in the room was Blake's gagging.

I looked down at Shoelink. "That was my fight. Why did you butt in?" I touched my chest, then made a fist and shook it at Mike Blake.

Shoelink ducked his head. "You, *Sangsu*." He touched his leg. "You make leg better. I your friend."

All I could do was stare at him, my self-appointed body-guard. With a shake of my head, I turned back to the bartender. "Two whiskeys, barkeep. If you please."

"Huh?" He tore his eyes from the writhing man on the floor. "Huh? Oh, yeah, yeah. Two whiskeys. Coming right up, sir." There was a note of respect in the bartender's voice now. One thing that never made any sense to me is why men can't just respect each other instead of having to demand the respect through strength or violence.

Shoelink laid his hand on my arm. "Please, *Sangsu*. No whiskey."

I frowned at him. This was the first time we'd been in a bar together, but I had just assumed he was like everyone else and hungering for a shot of halfway decent bourbon. "What do you want then, a beer?"

He shook his head. In his thin, singsong voice, he said. "No. No like beer. Sarsaparilla, please."

Another surprise. "Sarsaparilla? Is that what you want? Honest? Sarsaparilla?"

He nodded. "Whiskey make Zhou Gui Ling sick in belly." He made several elaborate gestures at his stomach. "Sarsaparilla is good, thank you."

"You heard him, bartender. Sarsaparilla."

"You bet. One sarsaparilla, coming right up."

By now, Blake had stopped gagging and was sitting up, still holding his throat tenderly. Two of the saloon patrons were squatting at his side, shooting menacing glances at us from the corner of their eyes.

The whiskey was far from bonded, but it was fiery and when it hit my stomach, it exploded in a blaze that warmed my entire lanky carcass. "One more."

Shoelink sipped his sarsaparilla.

I nodded the bartender over. "Any work around here?"

He eyed the two of us narrowly. "Winter ain't the best time to be ahuntin' jobs."

"Don't I reckon you're right." I sighed. "Still, I'd shore favor a warm bed and three squares a day. This ain't the best kind of weather for camping. I'm headin' for San Antone and try to hook up with a cattle drive this spring. Got a friend up in Dodge who staked out a small ranch up in the Tetons. I reckon on buying into it."

He frowned. "What about your friend, that old man?"

I shrugged. "What about him? Reckon he can do what he wants. I ain't his keeper." I patted my leg. "Though, I am obliged to him. Besides, from the look of that jasper on the floor, that *old man* can sure enough hold his own."

The bartender arched an eyebrow and shook his head. "Right off, I don't know of any work around for you, stranger. No offense intended, but for your friend there, I'm sure no one will put him on." He looked at his other patrons. "What about it, boys? Anyone looking for hands?"

A few mutters came from the room, none helpful. Suddenly, one jasper said. "What about Wash Cottle? He's always looking for hands."

The bartender frowned. "The Goat Ranch. Forget it. No self-respecting cowpoke is going to herd goats. Sheep is bad, but goats is worser."

I stopped him. "Hold on there, partner. Depending on the situation, there could be a time when a jasper's got to swallow some pride in order to get a full belly. Now, what about this Goat Ranch?"

One of the saloon patrons sidled up to the bar and eyed Shoelink. The diminutive Chinese wore the same dress as we did, except his feet were wrapped in some kind of cloth, and he wore a hat of some kind of black material that looked like a can turned upside down. In cold weather, he removed the sash he wore about his waist and tied it over the hat and under his chin.

I prompted the man. "Well, what about this Goat Ranch?"

"Well, Wash Cottle's got him a ranch about twenty miles south of here. Other side of the mountains. Easiest way is through Wild Rose Pass. The ranch is about half a mile beyond, right at Painted Comanche Tree. Wash runs a few thousand goats. Claims there's a market for them in

San Antone. Can't keep hands out there. Goats are contrarier than sheep and stink worse than a bunch of cowpokes at the end of a cattle drive.''

"But, you reckon he needs hands?"

The old man arched an eyebrow. "Could be. Can't say for sure, but could be." He nodded to the bartender. "Could be."

A ray of sunshine broke through the clouds and splashed across the floor of the saloon. I peered out the window. "Hate to travel in this snow. Didn't see no hotel. Reckon there's some place to spend the night?"

The bartender eyed Shoelink. "Him too?"

I clenched my teeth. I was growing right impatient with the man's snide looks, his snide remarks. "Yeah. Him too. You got something to say about it?"

The bartender clamped his mouth shut. The old man next to me spoke up. "Livery stable down the street. Elton will probably let you bunk in the hay if you put up your horse with him."

"Thanks. We might just do that." I finished my second whiskey and nodded to Shoelink. "Let's go get you a pony."

If I'd known then what the next twenty-four hours would start, I would have ridden right out of Hankering and not stopped until I reached San Antone.

Chapter Two

The snow melted fast that afternoon, but froze again when the night chill rolled in. Next morning, Shoelink and me was up with the sun. After sharing the hostler's breakfast of coffee and sourdough biscuits, we saddled up, me on Ned, and Shoelink astride the burro on which he had insisted.

Just before we rode out, the bartender pushed through the livery doors, his face grim. Tagging after him was a boy around ten or twelve with a piece of luggage in each hand. "Glad I found you old boys before you left. You still going to the Goat Ranch?"

I glanced at Shoelink, who just stared up at me, his hands folded at his waist. "I reckon we are."

He sighed with relief. "Good." He pulled the boy forward. "This here's Sam Cottle, Wash's son. Came in on the stage early this morning. Sure be obliged if you'd take him out to Wash, seeing as you're going out there anyway."

I studied the frail boy. His eyes were sunk deep in his head, and he appeared to have been crying. "He needs a pony."

"No problem." He spoke with the hostler, and while a pony was being rigged and the luggage tied down, the barkeep took me aside. "Bad news. The boy and his Ma was on the way out here, but she took sick this side of Fort

8

Worth and passed away. They buried her near Palo Pinto. Nobody knew what to do with the boy except send him on to his Pa.''

I looked at the boy, trying not to remember the emptiness I felt when my Pa died and left me all alone. The boy seemed lifeless, empty inside. ''Tough on the kid.''

The bartender just shrugged. ''Tell Wash he can bring the pony back in next time he comes to town.''

I shook my head. ''Forget it, partner. I'm a stranger hereabouts. No way I'm dropping off this little younker and telling his Pa that the boy's Ma died.''

''Yeah, reckon you got a point.'' The barkeep scratched his head. ''Tell you what. How about I write old Wash a letter? You just hand-deliver it to him. Tell him it's from Birt, the bartender. That work for you?''

I glanced at the boy standing next to the door like a lost puppy. I remembered being alone. I remembered the hurt. I remembered the pain. I sighed. ''Yeah.'' I nodded. ''I reckon that'll work okay.''

The bartender disappeared into the hostler's office. He returned minutes later with the note to the boy's pa. ''Here you are.'' He looked over his shoulder and lowered his voice. ''One other thing, stranger. Mike Blake ain't going to forget the stomping he took back in the saloon. And I reckon there's a bunch more old boys around Hankering who don't cotton to no China B . . . I mean, folks like Shoelink there hanging around town here.''

My voice grew cold. ''You feel that way too?''

He glanced at Shoelink and considered the question. ''Yeah. Blast it, I reckon I do.''

''Why you warning us then?''

Birt grinned sheepishly. ''Beats me. I guess I just hate to see folks taken advantage of.'' He hesitated, recognized the question in my eyes. "Even if I don't care for 'em, there ain't no sense in someone doing them dirty."

All I could do was stare at the man in wonder, puzzling over the human capability for being both bigoted and open-minded at the same time with a clear conscience. "Obliged." I glanced at the boy. "Climb aboard, son."

He looked up at me, his eyes all teary. "Yes, Sir."

With a click of my tongue, I sent Ned out of the stable. I felt mighty sorry for the younker.

The Goat Ranch was easy to find. We headed for the mountains on the horizon, found Wild Rose Pass, and finally reached the ranch just before dark. I glanced around, curious about the Painted Comanche Tree.

Wash Cottle stepped on the porch of the rock house and squinted at us. He blinked when he spotted the boy. His voice cracked. "Sam? Sampson?" He hurried across the hardpan. "Is that you, boy?"

Sam started bawling and slid off his pony. "Pa. Oh, Pa."

The rail-thin rancher hugged his son. "Boy, it shore is good to have you all here. I missed you and your Ma like all get-out." He looked around for his wife. "W . . . Where's your Ma, Boy? Where's Emily?"

"Here you are, Mr. Cottle." I handed him the note from the bartender. "This oughta explain things."

He took the note. "Who are you?" His eyes cut to Shoelink, then back to me.

"Just strangers passing through." Shoelink and me remained in our saddles. "Just strangers is all."

Wash eyed me suspiciously, then unfolded the note. He looked up at me once more, then began reading. He gasped. His shoulders sagged, and a tear rolled down his leathery cheek. Slowly, he crumpled the note and turned to his son.

The setting sun added a touch of strawberry red to the boy's sandy hair. Tears welled in his eyes.

Wash dropped to his knees in the mud and hugged the boy to him. Several long seconds passed. I watched the two, uncomfortable with such a personal display of pain and anguish.

Finally, Wash rose and squared his shoulders. He nodded to us. "Much obliged for your help. The bartender, Birt, he says you're looking for work." He put his hand around his son's shoulder and drew the boy into his side.

I nodded.

"Him too?" Wash looked at Shoelink.

"Him too. Unless the color of his skin bothers you."

Wash grinned wearily. "Mister, I learned long ago only to judge a man by what's inside him. Even if I did feel differently, right now, I got all the hurt and pain I can handle without looking for more." He paused. "What's your handle?"

"I'm Gil Vince. This here little feller I call Shoelink. That's the closest I can get to saying his Chinese name."

Shoelink nodded emphatically. He poked his chest. "Me Zhou Gui Ling." He dipped his head and folded his hands over his waist.

Wash Cottle studied us both, then turned to the house. "Put the animals in the corral and come on in. Beans and cornbread. Nothing fancy, but it'll stick to your ribs. Got an old red hound in the bar. Only got three legs. Name's Mutt, should he growl. Yell at him. He's a coward."

We did as he said. I noted the barn was unusual. The second floor had four gables, one facing in each direction. The corral covered three sides of the barn. We saw no sign of the cowardly hound, Mutt.

After grub in the main house, Shoelink and me headed

for the bunkhouse next door, where we built a fire in the potbellied stove and rolled out our blankets on the bunks.

I sat by the fire and rolled a cigarette. Warm fire, full belly, and a cigarette. All I needed was a cup of six-shooter coffee and I'd be in hog heaven.

While I sat and smoked, Shoelink, like every evening since we'd been together, pulled this little potbellied figure out of a cloth bag and set it on the floor at the end of the bunkhouse. He bowed over and placed his head on the floor in front of the figure. I wasn't at all sure of what he was up to, but I reckoned it had something to do with his religion.

I studied him. We were some pair, two cripples out in the middle of snow-covered country so desolate that buzzards only flew past once a month. Still, I wasn't complaining. Sitting there in the warmth of the wood stove sure beat bucking the icy wind and wet snow.

When he finished, Shoelink rose, bowed to me, and held up the little figure. "*Sangsu.*" He pointed to me and then to the figure. "*Sangsu.*" With another brief nod, he slipped into his bunk.

I blew out the lantern and lay back. The tip of my cigarette glowed a bright red in the darkness. Outside, the wind rattled the windowpanes. I stubbed out my cigarette on the puncheon floor and snuggled down in my blankets.

A light shone through the window. I propped up on my elbow and saw that the light came from a window in the ranch house. I padded across the cold floor to the window and rubbed a hole in the frost. A frown of pain knit my brows.

Not more than twenty feet away, Wash Cottle stood staring down at his sleeping son. Tears filled the man's eyes, and he gently rubbed his gnarled fingers across his boy's smooth cheek.

I tiptoed back to bed, ashamed to have seen such personal grief.

By noon the next day, the rest of the snow had melted, and I'd had my fill of goats. The old man back in the saloon was right. Goats were more stubborn than sin and smelled worse than six-day-old socks.

Beeves could be pushed by horses, sheep by dogs, but nothing could move those blasted goats. That's exactly what I told Wash at the dinner table that day. "Every time I took a step toward them, they faced me and ducked their heads, ready to charge me. Those blasted critters. And then when I tried to circle them, they just kept turning to face me. That old three-legged red hound of yours just sat and watched." I nodded to the slick-haired dog on the floor at Sam's feet. Like all boys, the younker had taken up with the hound right off.

Wash laughed. "What the Sam Hill was you trying to do anyway, Gil? Goats don't need a whole lot of tending."

I slathered butter on my cornbread and then soaked it with molasses. "I figured they needed water, so I started to push them down to the lake."

"I see." Wash winked at his boy. "Well, Gil, that was your first lesson. Goats don't push. They're not like sheep."

"Now you tell me. How do you get those mangy critters to go anywhere? That old hound there?"

The leathery rancher grinned. His light blue eyes twinkled in merriment. He glanced at the sleeping dog. "That old red hound is just to scare off coyotes and wolves at night. He doesn't try to push the goats anywhere."

I took a generous bite of cornbread and butter. "How'd he lose the leg?"

Wash grimaced and glanced at the door. "Don't know

for sure. I figure drunken cowpokes having fun. All I know
is Mutt came in one day with his front leg bleeding like
sin and hanging on by a piece of skin. I snipped the skin
and doctored the stump.'' He shook his head. ''He must
not have had more than a couple drops of blood left in him.
Why, I gave him up for dead. That old hound was mighty
sick for a couple weeks, but then he pulled right out, and
now he seems to get along on three legs as well as he did
with four.''

On the floor, Mutt whined in his sleep.

The leathery rancher chuckled. ''Mutt turned into a
smarter hound after that.''

I grinned. ''How's that?''

''Simple. Mutt learned that you guide goats, not push
'em. Before, he caused more trouble than he did good, scattering the goats and all. But he learned. You can too, Gil.
You just hang in here with me, and I'll sure enough make
you a goat man.''

''Goat man!'' I choked on the cornbread and gulped coffee to wash down the chunks. ''Not me, Wash. Not this
hombre. I ain't cut out for this kind of ranching. Beeves, I
know. But sheep and goats? It just ain't natural. Come
spring, I plan on joining up with a cattle drive up to Dodge.
I got an old partner who's found us a nice little spread in
the Tetons.''

Wash arched an eyebrow and hooked his thumb over his
shoulder to the north. ''The Goodnight-Loving Trail is back
that away.''

''Yep, but they go mostly to Denver. I'm going to try
the Western Trail to Dodge, and then maybe up on to
Ogallala.''

Beside me, Shoelink ate his cornbread and molasses in
tiny bites, like a bird. He kept his eyes on his plate while
Wash and me talked. Across the table, Sam just listened,

from time to time sneaking a glance at Shoelink or dropping a chunk of cornbread in front of the snoozing hound.

Wash arched an eyebrow. ''Sounds like you got things planned out good, Gil. I like a man who knows where he's going. So listen to me. I got a proposition that'll fit in with what you got in mind. A way to bring about a swap that'll do us both some good. Help you get what you want, and help me get what I want.''

A thunder of hooves interrupted us. Wash rose and headed for the door. Shoelink and me remained at the table, but I could see past Wash as the riders pulled up on the hardpan outside.

The hair on the back of my neck bristled.

The lead rider was Mike Blake, the hombre Shoelink had taken down a couple notches back in Hankering.

Chapter Three

The horses jittered around on the hardpan.

Wash cleared his throat and spoke cordially. "Howdy, Mike, Ray, Lem. Light and have some coffee."

Mike Blake shook his head. He jabbed a meaty finger at the house. "Cottle, you got that Chinese boy in there?"

Their horses stamped nervously.

The friendliness fled the rancher's voice. "Maybe. But, then, I don't reckon it's any of your business, Mike." Wash placed his hand on the doorjamb, as if to block their entry into the house.

Blake glanced at his two partners. "I'm making it my business, Cottle. We don't want none of them foreign people around here. This is white people's country."

Wash's voice rose. "Get out of here, Blake. You're on private property. You and your two hoodlum partners get off my place."

Faster than a flicker of light, Blake's six-gun leaped into his hand. "No Johnny-come-lately squatter can tell Mike Blake what to do. Why . . ."

I drew and fired in the same motion. My slug whipped under Wash's arm. Blake's hogleg ripped from his fingers.

"What the . . ." Blake screamed and grabbed his hand.

Quickly, I stepped past Wash onto the hardpan outside the door, my six-gun held steady on the three. "You best be able to back up your bluster, Blake. I've seen many a jasper end up in Boot Hill because their gun hand was no match for their big mouth.''

The other two hardcases eyed me warily. One's hand hesitated over his gun butt. I didn't give him a chance. I blew the handle off. He screamed and grabbed his waist, where slivers of wood and steel buried in his flesh. ''What about you?'' I turned the muzzle on the third.

He threw up his hands. ''Not me, mister. I'm just along for the ride.''

''All right, Blake. You heard Wash. Get out of here.''

His square face turned to rock. His black eyes blazed. His jaw clenched. ''I ain't forgettin' this, stranger. You neither, Cottle.''

I laughed. ''Just a warning, Blake. Come back, and you won't leave. Of course, I reckon you're probably too dumb to believe me, but I promise you. Cause Wash or Shoelink any more trouble, you'll be staring up at six feet of dirt with no idea how to crawl out.''

Angrily, Blake jerked his pony around and spurred it back toward Hankering. After the three riders disappeared, we went back to the table. The coffee was cold. Shoelink warmed it.

''Umm. Good.'' I took another sip, and then turned to Wash. ''Now, what was you was saying about some kind of swap?''

He shook his head. ''You ain't bad with that six-gun.''

Before I could reply, Sam spoke up. ''Yeah. I betcha you're faster than anything.'' He looked up at his Pa. ''That's what I want be, Pa. Fast with a gun.''

I shook my head. ''No, you don't, Sam. A fast gunnie has only two things to look forward to. One is more fast guns coming after him.''

The youngster nodded eagerly. ''What's the other?''

''An early grave.''

For a moment, the boy frowned, then nodded slowly.

"Mr. Vince is right, son," said Wash. "You need to learn how to use a gun, but what's more important, you best learn when to use it."

"Listen to your pa, boy. Now, Wash, what was this swap business you were talking about?"

Wash frowned at me momentarily. "Oh, yeah, yeah. What I was saying, Gil, was that I got a proposition that will do us both some good."

I eyed him suspiciously. No one had ever done me any favors, and I figured Wash Cottle was looking out for himself, but I wasn't born in the woods to be scared by an owl, so I decided to give him my ear. "What do you have in mind?"

He looked at his boy, then leaned his elbows on the rough table and stared me square in the eyes. "You two boys, especially the old Oriental gentleman, need a place for the winter. Come spring, I plan to push more than two thousand goats to San Antone. I need help for that. Take about thirty days."

"Yes, sir." I chuckled, remembering just how contrary those goats were. "I reckon you sure do need help if you're crazy enough to try."

Wash ignored my sarcasm. He continued. "Spend the winter here. Help around the place. Learn about the goats, and when we reach San Antone, I'll pay each of you thirty dollars a month. That'll be for about five months. Once we hit San Antone, you can hook on to a cattle drive up to Dodge. That ought to be about the middle of the season."

He paused, took a deep breath, and released it noisily. "What do you think?"

Anyway I turned the offer, I came out ahead. I needed a bunk for the winter; I planned to go to San Antone anyway; and I would end up with a pocketful of Yankee dollars to add to the money I made pushing beeves to Dodge. Not bad.

"Him too?" I dipped my head toward Shoelink.

Wash nodded. "Him too."

"What about it, Shoelink? You game?"

The little Chinese feller frowned at my question. He tapped his chest, then gestured to me. "Zhou Gui Ling stay with *Sangsu*." He eyed me a moment as if to say that was the end of the discussion, and then he turned back to his cornbread.

"He thinks a powerful lot of you, Gil." Wash said.

I poured some more coffee. "Goes both ways. He busted a leg when he was with the Comanches. I found him and took care of him. Two days after he was hobbling around on crutches, a diamondback got me." I patted my leg. "Shoelink knew exactly what to do." I chuckled and rolled a cigarette. "We took turns helping each other out." I touched a match to the paper. It flared, and I inhaled, savoring the taste of the smoke.

"That's why you both limp, huh?"

"Yeah. We got to be careful though."

"Why's that?"

"If we walk side by side, we keep bumping in to each other."

Wash frowned, then grinned. "Yeah. I reckon you would." He paused and cut his eyes toward Shoelink. He arched an eyebrow at the Oriental's white hair. "Look. I don't mean nothing by this, but can that old gentleman handle the trip?"

A sly grin crinkled my lips. "That old gentleman is a young man. Maybe twenty-five or so."

Wash eyed me skeptically.

I explained. "When I tended his broke leg, I realized he was a young man. His leg is muscular and smooth, like a young man's. Best I can decipher from his jabbering, he came over here back in the sixties to help build the railroads, but up on the plains, he was captured by Indians. I reckon maybe Ute or Pawnee or even Arapaho. They swapped him to the Comanche, who made a pet out of him until he busted a leg. They went off and left him. That's when I came along.''

Wash sipped his coffee and eyed Shoelink, who continued to nibble at his meal. ''But his hair, it's white as snow.''

''Turned like that with the Injuns. Best I gather, they never hurt him, but they was so savage-looking and all, they just terrified the little feller to pieces.''

The leathery faced rancher studied the little Oriental. ''What's the name he calls you mean? What is it . . . *Sangsu*?''

I remembered the night before. ''He's got some kind of religious figure. He called it *Sangsu*.'' I hesitated. My ears burned slightly. ''But then, a while back, we ran across a herd of beeves. He said *Sangsu* and pointed at the lead steer and then at me.'' With a chuckle, I patted my lean belly. ''I can't figure it out. I sure don't have the stomach on me that his little doll has. Maybe he thinks I'm just a hard-headed mossback.''

''I doubt that.'' Wash laughed.

''Anyway, I just figured it would be a heap easier for me to understand him. Reckon he's got enough trouble with our language.''

''Well, I swan. I've read about Chinese folks, but I never met any. The railroads sure brought a lot of them over here, didn't they?''

''That's what I heard.'' I shrugged. ''I never paid much attention.''

Wash paused. ''Well, back to what we were talking

about. What do you think of my offer? Stay here the winter, help push the goats to market, and then hook onto a cattle drive that'll take you up to that ranch in the Tetons?''

''Might as well. Like you say, we're looking for a winter bunk. Besides, you make good coffee.''

''We got a deal then.''

''I reckon. You got a brand?''

''Don't need one.'' He grinned slyly.

''Huh?''

''That's right. Who else around here's got goats?''

He had me there. I chuckled. ''All right, but tell me. Who do you plan on selling these miserable critters to? No way I can see a jasper making money out of them.''

A sly grin crinkled his face. ''You like that butter?''

I frowned down at the butter-and molasses-soaked cornbread on my plate. ''Yeah. It's right tasty. Why?''

''Goat butter.''

My mouth twisted. ''Goat butter?''

He made a gesture to the east. ''A few years back, someone developed a product called oleomargarine . . . about 1868. It's gone over big, created a market for butters. They claim goat butter is tops. A cattle broker in San Antone is paying three dollars a head for goats. I got over two thousand ready to go, and another three, maybe four hundred here for the next crop. A doe, that's the female goat, usually drops twins, and in eight months, the twins will be ready. In three years, a single doe can be responsible for ninety offspring. With that kind of production, every two years I'll have another twenty-five hundred ready to go. That's around seventy-five hundred dollars every couple years.''

He hesitated and grinned over at Sam, who was playing with Mutt. ''At that rate,'' he added. ''In a few years, Sam and me can build ourselves a fine little spread here.''

I whistled, skeptical of any venture being so successful. "What if the demand is gone by then?"

Wash shrugged. "The market won't dry up. People from all over the world are coming into the East. New York and Philadelphia and all those big cities up there are busting opening with newcomers. Even if milk or butter or both lost their markets, goat meat is considered a delicacy in many places."

"A what?"

"Delicacy. You know, right tasty. Like beefsteak."

I shook my head. "I know the Mexicans like goat, *cabra*, they call it, but I don't figure goat meat would taste nothing like beefsteak."

Wash laughed. "You're right about that, but then, there's no accounting for people's taste. Some folks like it better than beefsteak."

"I don't know. Sure seems like a gamble to me."

"Everything's a gamble, Gil. You wake up in the morning and you're gambling that you'll be alive that night. A man can't stop trying just because something might happen."

He was right, I had to admit. Life was a gamble.

The next morning, Washington Isaac Cottle broke his neck.

Chapter Four

Just before sunrise, Shoelink and me climbed from our bunks. As I jumped into my pants and boots, I heard a horse ride away. I glanced out the window and saw Wash Cottle silhouetted against the brilliant red of the rising sun, heading toward town. I watched until he disappeared into Wild Rose Pass to the north, then I finished dressing.

A pot of steaming coffee and a pan of cornbread sat on the stove. A note leaned up against the jar of molasses.

> Boys,
> Gone to Hankering. Need supplies.
> Back before dark.
> Washington Cottle

Wash must've rose earlier, for the cornbread was fresh-baked. I sliced open a slab, heaped a chunk of goat butter on it, and watched as the hot bread melted the pale butter.

For a few seconds, I reconsidered my own plans. Maybe this was the home I'd been looking for instead of that wild dream about the Tetons. If Wash's plan came true, he'd need a permanent hand around here, and I reckoned I could learn about goats if I put my mind to it. At least until I could build up a grubstake that would let me start my own place.

Just as quickly, I dismissed the idea. The deal Wash and

23

me had worked out was just dandy. And the plans I had were already in place. No sense in changing anything.

We were just finishing up breakfast when Wash's dun came limping in, holding its front left off the ground. "What the blazes," I muttered, grabbing my hat and rushing for the door.

Shoelink stayed on my heels.

I knelt and ran my fingers gingerly over the dun's pastern and fetlock. I winced. Broken. My blood ran cold.

After leading the dun into the barn, I unsaddled him and threw a rig on my roan. I turned to Shoelink. "Wash might be hurt. Look after the boy. I'll be back as soon as I can."

Shoelink nodded.

Five miles out, I found Wash Cottle in the middle of a prairie dog town. He lay on his back, his head twisted at an unnatural angle. The sign was easy to read. The dun had been in a running two-step gait, a comfortable lope that ate up the miles. The pony stepped in a hole and sent Washington Cottle over his head.

We buried Wash on the ranch a short piece from the house. His neighbors at the Circle W on one side, the Box Slash on the other, and a handful of townsfolk showed up.

After the funeral, Sam stood staring down at his pa's grave. Mutt crawled on the fresh soil and lay motionless. I returned to the kitchen. Parson Tomlinson and Joshua Curtice, the owner of the Circle W, which adjoined Wash's place at Wild Rose Pass on the east side, followed me.

Shoelink poured us some coffee. We stared silently out the window as Joshua's daughter, Margaret, consoled Sam by the grave. She looked to be in her early twenties, and I wondered why some jasper hadn't already thrown a loop around her.

"What do you figure on doing with the boy, Mr. Vince?" The parson looked at me.

I shifted my feet uncomfortably. I hadn't considered the boy. He wasn't my business. What I'd really figured to do, now that Wash was planted, was to ride on out. The preacher's question caught me off guard. "Well, Parson, it don't seem like I'm really the one to have the say-so. I just met Wash a couple days back."

Joshua Curtice produced a flask from his coat pocket and splashed a dollop of whiskey in his cup and then offered it to me. I glanced at the parson, then nodded. "Sorry, Parson," Joshua said. "But my old bones stay chilled all winter. I need the warmth."

Without waiting for the parson to reply, Joshua turned to me. "You worked for Wash." He said it like he expected me to step right in and take over everything.

"Yeah, but only for a couple days."

The older man shrugged. "You know what he had in mind for the ranch here?"

"Reckon I do."

Margaret came back in, leaving Sam and Mutt at the grave. Her eyes were sad. "He'll be in directly."

We all nodded. I stared at my coffee.

Joshua broke the silence. "What about it, Gil? You was going to tell us what Wash had in mind for the ranch."

"Yeah." I nodded to the southeast. "Well, he wanted to take two thousand goats to San Antone." With Margaret listening, I quickly outlined the rest of his plans to the two men.

Joshua smoothed his handlebar mustache that was the same color gray as his shoulder-length hair. "You know anything about goats, Gil?"

Margaret arched a curious eyebrow. She was sure pleasant to look at. She smiled. I went dumb.

"Gil. You hear? You know anything about goats?"

"Huh?" I jerked around. "No, sir. I don't know the first thing about goats except you can't drive 'em like beeves. Wash was going to teach me, but . . ."

A heavy silence fell over the room. Outside, the clouds broke and a shaft of sunlight splashed through the window, brightening the room. Joshua cleared his throat. In his deep bass voice, he said, "You reckon you can do what Wash wanted, Gil?"

I glanced at Shoelink, who stood beside the stove, looking at me. His expression didn't change, but I had the feeling he was hoping I'd say yes. Personally, I wasn't any too anxious to get that involved, to take Wash's whole crazy scheme on my own shoulders. The entire situation was different now. The smart move for me was to roll up my soogan and head out.

I met Parson Tomlinson's questioning gaze, then turned to Joshua. "I don't know, Mr. Curtice."

Margaret's smile faded into frown.

Hastily I added. "But I reckon I could, were I a mind to."

"It's a far piece to San Antone, almost three hundred miles." Joshua frowned.

"Wash figured he could get them there." Then, to my own horror, I heard the next words come from my lips. "If Wash thought he could get them through, I can too."

Margaret's smile returned.

I cursed my own foolish vanity. I'd dug myself a hole too blasted deep to climb out of.

The old rancher studied me several seconds, like he was trying to peer deep inside my head to see what made me tick. Finally, he turned to the parson. "Preacher, I think we ought to give Gil a chance. By all rights, this here ranch is the boy's now. No sense in lettin' all Wash's work go for nothing. I say, let Gil swing the axe at it . . . with the same deal he made with Wash. That way, the boy'll have something to keep him going."

Parson Tomlinson considered Joshua's words. "Don't seem too fair. I mean, just to give Gil the same agreement he had with Wash. If Gil does agree, his work is doubled now."

I'd never realized until then the foolish things a man can say just to impress a woman. "No, sir. No change. A deal's a deal."

Later, I would admit just what a moronic remark I made, but at the time, my idiocy was suppressed by the buttons popping off my shirt when Margaret Curtice smiled and thanked me. "You are a very generous and caring man, Mr. Vince."

I choked on my reply. All I could do was nod. Still, I reminded myself that I was still going to San Antone, and I could still hook on to a cattle drive up to Dodge, and I would still be able to buy into the ranch in the Tetons.

She shot her Pa a glance; they stared up at me. She cleared her throat. "I really think Sampson should come back to the ranch with Pa and me. A young boy needs understanding and sympathy at a time like this."

Joshua Curtice studied the ground at his feet mighty hard.

I shrugged, stung by the implication in her words. "Well, if Sam wants to, Ma'am, that's fine with me. However, I don't see no reason he won't get the same understanding here," I added. "Besides, his dog's here."

That was a mistake. Her eyes turned cold. "All I mean, Mr. Vince," she replied curtly. "Is that he needs a woman's touch now, not the rough and tough understanding of drifters. And we can take the dog with us."

Her Pa spoke up. "Margaret. Mind your manners."

Her eyes blazed. "You said so yourself, Pa. The boy needs a stable home, not . . ." She hesitated, then thought better of what she was going to say.

Joshua grinned sheepishly at me. "The girl's right, Gil. The boy would be better off with us. You and the Chinese boy, you're good men, but you don't know nothing about boys."

My dander was up. I eyed Margaret coldly. "I reckon I know as much about boys as a spinster woman, Mr. Curtice."

Now I was in trouble. That was the wrong thing to say.

Margaret's eyes bugged open. Her cheeks turned red as a West Texas prairie fire. She glared at me for a moment, then her face crumpled into tears and she ran out to the buggy.

I groaned and shook my head. "Sorry, Mr. Curtice. I wouldn't blame you if you took a poke at me. I just got a big mouth at times. Miss Margaret just rubbed me the wrong way. Naturally, if Sam wants to go, he can. I ain't got the right to say nothing one way or another. She's right. I'm only a drifter."

The old rancher studied me a moment, then glanced out the door at his daughter. He sighed. "Raising a girl without her ma is quite a chore, Gil. Maybe I protect her too much. I reckon she's got to learn that sometimes she's going to get back more than she gives."

We looked into each other's eyes for several seconds. We understood each other. I offered my hand. "Much obliged."

He took my hand.

"I don't know, Joshua," said Parson Tomlinson. "I still think the boy would be better off with Margaret and you."

Sam dropped to his knees and put his arms around Mutt's neck. "No. I want to stay here. I won't go."

Joshua frowned at the Parson. "No sense in upsettin' the boy no more. Maybe tomorrow, he'll come in." The old rancher looked at me.

"The boy'll be fine, Joshua. He gets lonely, we'll fetch him to you." I glanced toward the buggy. "Tell your daughter that, if you don't mind."

"Sounds good to me." He gestured to the table filled with covered dishes. "You boys won't have to do no cooking for a spell."

"We got enough for a week." I laughed, but I wasn't happy. I'd committed myself to a Herculean task, one I wasn't too sure I could handle.

Chapter Five

A pallor of gloom hung over the ranch after everyone left.

The remainder of the day, Sam sat on the ground by his pa's grave with Mutt at his side, ignoring the cold wind whipping down through Wild Rose Pass.

Shoelink filled a plate with fried chicken, dumplings and gravy, succotash, and biscuits, but the boy only nibbled. Mutt cleaned the plate.

I ambled out to the corral, trying to sort the confusion in my head, regretting my show of bravado. I'd really bucked the tiger this time. And lost. Only an idiot would agree to take two thousand goats, ornery critters that refused to be herded, to San Antone across three hundred miles of prairie, scrub oak forests, rocky mountains, and treacherous rivers. Never mind the mountain lions and bears and wolves. The wild animals were merely an extra topping to my unpleasant dish.

The sun shone brightly, but the cold wind cut through my duds, chilling me to the bone. The corral looked out over miles of mesquite and bunchgrass. Great herds of goats milled about behind the walls of stone Wash had stacked to break the wind.

Not many of the critters were browsing, instead opting to stay out of the cold. "Maybe you critters aren't so dumb, after all," I said.

30

When the goats spotted me, they started moving, a slow rolling wave of white and brown from across the prairie. Behind me, the barn bulged with wild grass Wash had cut and stacked. I knew enough about beeves to realize the goats expected some grub, so I climbed up in the hayloft and forked several bundles of grass to the corral below.

"Take it easy, you greedy little critters." The goats at the rear pressed in on the ones in front, shoving them into the side of the barn.

I felt a hand on my arm.

Shoelink crooked his finger. "Here, *Sangsu*. See."

He led me a quarter of the way around the second floor and threw open the doors on the second side of the barn. Instantly, I realized Wash's purpose in building such an unusual structure. He could feed the goats from three sides.

The little Oriental grabbed a pitchfork and motioned me to the third door as he began forking hay to the goats. Quickly, I did the same on the third side.

After a few minutes, Shoelink approached. He peered out my window and shook his head. "Too much." He wagged a skinny finger back and forth, then signaled for me to accompany him. "Here, *Sangsu*."

On his side, the goats were cleaning up the last of the wild grass. On my side, piles remained. "Goats . . ." He struggled to find the words. "Goats eat little . . . what they need. No fill."

I frowned. "Fill?"

He grimaced, then patted his stomach. "Fill. Goats stop when fill." He tapped his skull. "Goats wise."

His words cheered me. I pointed at him. "You know goats?"

He nodded. "My . . . honorable father and his honorable father raise fine goats. Much milk, much cheese. Much meat." He licked his lips in the first display of emotion I had seen from him.

For the first time since the funeral, I felt a surge of hope. "Can you herd them to San Antone?"

"San . . . Antone?" He frowned and cocked his head to one side.

"A town . . . a town about three hundr . . ." I paused. No sense in explaining all that to him. He wouldn't understand it anyway. "Can you . . ." I pointed at his chest, then at the goats, and then made a pushing motion with my hands to the southeast. "Move goat."

He looked at his chest, at the goats, to the southeast. A quick nod. *"Ai."*

I stared at him a moment. I didn't believe him. Every time I got close to those contrary animals, they scooted around and lowered their heads, ready to run over me if I so much as said boo. I held my hands out to my side. "How?"

For a moment, he stared at me blankly. Then his eyes lit with understanding. He held up a finger and stared down at the goats. I followed his gaze, but saw nothing except goats. Abruptly, he nodded. "Come." He crooked a finger and padded on tiptoe across the loft to the ladder.

On the ground, he removed the sash about his waist and pushed through the milling goats to an old doe, about forty inches high with a coat of rusty white. She turned her head as he approached. Gently, he slipped the sash around her neck and tightened it.

Choking the poor animal won't help, I thought to myself.

"Come, *Sangsu*. We go."

Before I could take a step, Shoelink broke into a funny little song and led off across the prairie in his padding, two-step, tiptoe walk. The doe followed, like a puppy. And one by one, the entire herd fell in behind.

I stared in astonishment at the parade of goats winding across the windswept prairie. Impossible. But there it was. "Well, I swan." That's all I could say. "Well, I swan."

In the distance, a handful of riders appeared on the horizon. I watched curiously as they rode toward the ranch. As they drew closer, I saw the lead rider was John Howard, the patriarch of the Slash Bar on the west side of Wash's ranch. A handful of tough-looking hombres rode with him, gunnies, if I'd ever seen any.

He pulled up and nodded. "Howdy."

"Mr. Howard." I pointed to the ranch house. "Hot coffee."

"No, thanks." He shook his head sharply. "This is business, Mr. Vince. I'll get right to the point. I want to buy Cottle's place. I hear from the preacher you're running it for the boy, so I'm willing to make him a fair price."

I considered his words. "Don't reckon I can answer for the boy, Mr. Howard. I can talk to him and give him your offer."

Howard winced. "He's just a boy. He ain't got no business sense. You're the one."

"But the ranch is his."

His cheeks reddened, but he held his temper. "Wash Cottle doesn't hold title to all this land, only about half of it."

That announcement came as a surprise to me, but I tried not to show it. I lied. "He told me."

Howard's eyes widened, then narrowed warily. "Reckon you two was mighty close."

The first lie worked. Might as well try another one. Keep the old rancher off guard. "No. After his death, me and the boy went through his papers. That's when I realized he only owned half of the place," I said, throwing his words back in his face.

Before he could reply, I continued. "Give me your offer, Mr. Howard. I'll pass it on to the boy. I want the boy taken care of. He ain't no kin of mine, but I like the younker. If the offer's fair, I'll recommend he take it."

The old man studied me, like a rogue wolf ready to pounce. I could see the calculating going on his head. "He's got twenty sections here, half under title. I'll give him a dollar an acre for the titled land. That comes to—"

"Six thousand, four hundred," I said, interrupting.

"Huh? Why, yeah. Yeah. Six thousand, four hundred. That's right."

I took a step back and raised my hand to say adios. "Appreciate you dropping by, Mr. Howard. Soon as the boy and me talk, I'll get back to you."

For a moment, the elderly rancher was taken aback by my abrupt dismissal. From the expression on his face, he was used to beckoning and dismissing, not the other way around. He glanced sheepishly at his men, but their eyes remained on me, not a one of them picking up the undercurrent of our conversation.

"Sure." He nodded. "You do that. Just don't wait too long. The offer ain't good forever."

I took another step back. "I understand, Mr. Howard. You can be sure we'll talk about it right soon and get back with you."

That night, I did exactly what I told John Howard I had already done. I dug through the papers Wash Cottle kept in a wooden box next to the regulator clock on the fireplace mantel. I'd seen the box before, but hated to pry into another man's business.

Now, I had no choice. I set the box on the crossbuck table and poured a cup of extra strong six-shooter coffee and rolled a cigarette.

Sure enough, Howard was right. As I studied the layout of the ranch, I couldn't help smiling at Wash Cottle's skill at adapting both the Union Pacific and Central Pacific Railroad's unorthodox land purchases to his own purpose.

His twenty-section ranch was rectangular, and he had purchased title to eleven sections, all either on water or grass, leaving nine sections of rough country thick with scrub and rocks that no squatter would dream of chancing, yet the browse on those nine sections were ideal graze for goats as well as inaccessible except over titled land.

I leaned back and stretched, my eyes on the papers unfolded on the table before me. I grinned. "I gotta hand it to you, Wash. You knew how to deal the cards in your favor."

Two days later, we refused John Howard's offer.

He glowered, and the expression in his eyes told me we had not heard the last of the old rancher. Talk around Hankering, especially in Birt's saloon, reinforced my hunch. John Howard was used to getting his way.

The hair on the back of my neck tingled. Seemed like every time I turned around, I was getting in a mite deeper.

Two weeks later, a band of night riders made a lightning run at the ranch, peppering the rock walls with slugs, then disappearing into the night before I could grab my Winchester and return fire.

None of us were hurt, but we couldn't find Mutt. "Blast," I muttered, hoping the worthless old red hound wasn't dead. He wasn't. I found him hiding in a hole he'd dug under the bunkhouse. It was two days before he came out. I shook my head at him. "Wash was right. You're a big coward."

He ambled forward, wagging his tail and trying to rub his head against my leg.

I growled. "Don't try to get on my good side, you mangy old critter." At the same time, I reached down and scratched behind his ears.

Word in town was that Mike Blake was behind the raid. Without proof, I couldn't confront him. All I could do was wait.

I made sure Sam's bunk was behind solid rock with no chance of a ricochet. I slept with the Winchester at my bunk.

A week later, the riders hit us again, and again they swept through before I could get off a well-aimed shot.

"Blake's trying to get us rankled."

Both Sam and Shoelink frowned at me. Neither understood what I meant, for I hadn't discussed the situation with them. I knew I couldn't get any help from town out there, so we were the ones who would have to stop the raids.

I puzzled for a solution. What about an ambush, a one-man ambush?

Forget it.

Then, I had an idea.

Over breakfast the next morning, I laid it out for Sam and Shoelink.

"Both times the riders came in from the south, hit the ranch, and headed out through Wild Rose Pass. Well, next time they come, we'll have a surprise for them."

I went on to explain, after which we rolled up our sleeves and got busy.

Halfway through the pass was a sharp decline in the trail where the riders had to slow or go head over heels. We laid a rope across the trail so that we could jerk it neck-high as they rode through. On the sandstone cliffs on either side of the trail, we propped up timbers upon which we piled stones and attached trip ropes.

Farther back down the pass toward the ranch, we built a

pyre of dry grass and brittle mesquite on the rim of one of the ledges overlooking the pass.

The plan was simple. Use the fire to drive the riders into the rock slides.

And now, all we had to do was wait.

For four long, cold nights we waited; on the fifth, the riders returned.

As the previous two times, they swept through the ranch, throwing lead at the ranch house, then highballing for Wild Rose Pass.

As soon as I heard the gunfire, I yanked the rope tight, neck-high across the pass, and cinched the end to a stump. I glanced at the rim a quarter of a mile back. A flicker of fire appeared.

Hoofbeats grew closer.

Suddenly, the pyre on the rim exploded into a ball of flames and came hurtling down the precipice onto the trail. I crossed my fingers, hoping Sam and Shoelink had timed the fire right.

Wild screams and frightened shouts told me Sam and Shoelink's timing had been perfect. The night riders spurred their horses forward in a desperate effort to escape the ball of fire. Their attention was focused behind.

The three in the lead hit the rope and somersaulted backward off their ponies. The other riders pulled up, and milled about in confusion. At the same time, the impact on the rope yanked the trip ropes holding the stones.

Seconds later, the thunder of a landslide filled the night, smothering out the shouts and screams of the night riders.

The next day in Hankering, several cowpokes stumbled around with broken arms and legs. Mike Blake's gun hand was bandaged heavily. Rumor was, he lost three fingers on the hand.

The night riders never bothered us anymore that winter.

Chapter Six

The remainder of the winter passed slowly. Joshua Curtice dropped by from time to time, but his daughter never accompanied him. "I'm afraid you got yourself an enemy for life, Gil," he remarked one blustery day while we sat at the crossbuck table sipping six-shooter coffee laced with store-bought whiskey.

I tried not to show my disappointment. "Well, I'm right sorry about that, Mr. Curtice, but since I don't reckon there's much I can do about it, I won't let it worry me."

He chuckled. "That's about all you can do." He pulled out his flask and doubly reinforced our coffee. "By the way, you heard any more from John Howard?"

"About this place?" I shook my head. "Nope. He stopped by once to see how we were doing, but he didn't make any mention of wanting the ranch."

Joshua grimaced and sipped gingerly at his steaming coffee. "That don't sound like John. Usually, he keeps after what he wants until he gets it."

I grunted. "Reckon every jasper is bound to be disappointed at one time or another."

"Reckon so." The old rancher smoothed his handlebar mustache. "Just don't you let down your guard. I've knowed John for thirty years. I'd bet the tiger he ain't finished."

"Makes sense. By the way," I said, changing the subject, "Last November, one of the saloon regulars mentioned a tree out here. I was going to ask Wash about it, but . . . well . . . I never got the chance."

"You mean Painted Comanche Tree?"

"Yeah. That's it. Is it really a tree?"

Joshua laughed. "You bet. Biggest sycamore I ever saw. You know that pond about half a mile south of here?" I nodded. "It's down there. Years back, so the story goes, Comanches stopped off at the pond during their travels. The first drew some pictures on the trunk. After that, other Comanches started recording a history of sorts on the trunk of the tree, using their paints."

"A history?"

"Yeah. Not like in a book, but in pictures. Sort of a story of their lives."

I shook my head. "I'd like to see that."

Joshua nodded. "It's a sight. I can't read it, but word is that some of the pictures are over a hundred years old." He arched an eyebrow. " 'Course, that's hard for an old skeptic like me to believe, but then, that's the story."

As soon as Joshua Curtice left, I saddled up and rode down to the pond. There was the tree, a sycamore, a big one. The pictures were weathered and faded, but I could make out some that depicted buffalo hunts, one or two battles, then a couple celebrations of some sort. Then there was one with several wickiups around a fire and small figures, kids I guessed, playing some kind of game.

As the days passed, I was gradually coming to terms with myself about the commitment I'd made to get the herd to San Antonio, foolish or not. A man agrees to try, he's got to try, so I settled down to make the best of what I considered a bad situation.

And to add to my gloomy predicament, the weather decided to take a hand. West Texas winters are a confusing mixture of uncertainty—a blizzard one day, and a scorcher the next. But for the most part, the weather was cold, biting, and bitter.

Just after New Years, Margaret Curtice and her pa, Joshua, stopped by with Parson Tomlinson and his wife. She tried to talk Sam into going back to the ranch for a short visit with her and her pa. "To get away from batching it like this," she said, trying to sound light and gay. "Just men. You're bound to be hungry for a good meal."

Sam shook his head, his blond hair approaching shoulder length by now. "No, Ma'am. Shoelink, he whips us up some dandy grub. Why last night, we had fresh biscuits and Chunking goulash."

Margaret wrinkled her nose. "Chunking goulash. What on earth is that?"

I chuckled. "That's what we call it. Venison and potatoes in a thick gravy."

"Yes, Ma'am," Sam added. "And it's real fine when you sop the biscuits in the gravy."

Joshua Curtice licked his lips.

Margaret frowned at me. I had the feeling she was disappointed that we were managing so well, and I know she was upset because Sam refused again. "Potatoes? Where did you get potatoes this time of year?"

"Shoelink." I hooked my thumb at the diminutive Oriental man who sat quietly at the end of the table. "You know that pond down on the south side of the mountains, where Painted Comanche Tree is?"

"Yes."

"Well, Shoelink spent time with the Comanches. He learned how they cooked, so he went down there and found some wild plants called plantain. Taste just like potatoes."

"Sounds good." Joshua patted his ample belly.

"We'd offer you some, but we ate it all."

Joshua roared. "Don't sound to me they're starving, Margaret. Satisfied?"

She hid her disappointment well. She sniffed. "Yes, Pa." She turned her back on me and spoke directly to Sam. "Remember, Sam, anytime you want to come for a visit, come ahead."

He grinned. "I will."

And I knew the younker meant it, but that period of time in Texas was like a circus for boys. Mountains, prairies, wild game, fish, and for Sam, the time and freedom to enjoy it all.

And like all boys, Sam quickly took to the excitement of the open prairie, though some nights I heard him snuffling in his bed after the lanterns were out. Come morning, however, he was raring to go.

With Mutt at his side, there were mountains to climb, prairies to cross, deer to hunt, and fish to catch, though the rough weather made the latter chancy.

I learned a lot about goats during those cold, miserable days, some from the few booklets and notes Wash left behind, but mainly from the animals themselves. Goats might be contrary, but they weren't dumb like beeves. While the addle-brained beeves stood out in the middle of the rain and snow, goats congregated in shelters, behind walls, under ledges, out of the weather like anyone with good sense. They hated rain, and on several occasions, I noticed they had already gathered in shelter even before the storm struck.

Every day, I rode out over the twenty square miles of ranch land Wash had settled. Some days, Shoelink accompanied me on his burro to gather sundry herbs as well as mesquite bean-pods, wild squash, onions, and other wild plants to add to our meals. Other days, Sam tagged along on a dun pony we'd bought in Hankering. But each day I rode the ranch, Mutt followed, leaving Sam despite the boy's urging the hound to remain behind.

Mutt would run off a few feet, halt, look back, then dash after me for another several yards, then repeat the whole process all over again until finally we were out of sight.

Sam and me talked about the hound's behavior one night at supper while Shoelink listened on. "All I can figure, Sam, is that your pa and Mutt spent so much time together, the hound knew what was really important to Wash, and he wants to make it all come true."

A frown knit the boy's forehead. "You really think so, Gil? I mean, you believe dogs can think like that?"

I studied the boy. Gone was the pale, sickly complexion of the young man who had come out back in the autumn. Sam's face was weathered, ruddy with exposure to the wind and snow, a typical young westerner. "I don't know, Sam. All I know is, there was something special between that hound and your pa."

He considered my reply for several seconds, then nodded. "Maybe so."

Together, Sam and me learned goats the hard way, by trial and error. We recognized they could survive on bushes, trees, desert scrub, and herbs when cattle and sheep would starve. That explained why Wash had stored no more hay than he had.

From the pamphlets, we learned that the critters I had been calling bulls and heifers were really bucks and does, like deer, but it was a nose-wrenching experience that taught us it was the buck that smelled. Why, I never could figure out, but whenever I came upon a herd of bucks, the smell almost knocked me out of my saddle.

One day, Sam and me sat on our ponies beside Painted Comanche Tree, staring at the faded designs decorating the trunk of the huge sycamore. Mutt waded into the water and drank deeply.

"Indians do all that, Gil?"

"Yep." I reached for my bag of Durham, then realized I was out. Had been for a month. Might as well quit. "I can't read all those pictures, but they tell a story . . . you know, like all of that stick writing that comes from Egypt. Only right smart hombres can read that kind of writing. Like that picture there," I said, pointing to the painted scene depicting wigwams around the fire and the children playing some kind of game. "I'd like to be able to understand what the Injuns were trying to tell us."

Sam looked up at me, his once pale face glowing with health after months of exposure to the weather and hard work on the ranch. Despite the fact the goats didn't need much tending, there were chores to be done. "I bet my pa could read it."

"I reckon he could. From all I know, your pa was a smart man. He went to some place back east called a college. I reckon that has something to do with schooling." I hesitated, grinned down at the boy. "Which reminds me. You need some schooling. I reckon when me and Shoelink head out with the goats, we'll leave you and Mutt with the Curtices so you can go to school."

His grin faded. "Awww. I don't need no schooling, Gil. I can read and cipher."

"Maybe so, youngster, but education is important and getting more important every day. Your pa knew that. All these papers he had about the goats shows he was trying to learn from other jaspers too. Reckon he knew that a hombre can't ever have too much learning. And the way he went about buying this ranch here. Why, no average cowpoke like me could have done it."

Sam frowned up at me. "What do you mean?"

I grimaced, unsure if I could explain it proper. "Well, he studied the countryside and learned that there were patches of land that was no good without the patch next to it. If he bought the good patch, he could use the other one because no one else would want it." I hesitated, not really certain I understood what I was saying myself.

His frown deepened. "I don't understand."

Right then, I saw a chance to encourage him to take more schooling. "Well, you see . . . that's just what I've been saying. If you had more schooling, you would understand . . . like your pa." It was a white lie, but I didn't reckon anyone would mind if it helped the younker get more education.

Sam considered what I said. "I could learn on the way to San Antone."

I studied the boy. In the last few months, he'd put on about twenty pounds and three inches. He was still about five inches below me, but sprouting like he was, within a year, he'd pass me by. "Look, Sam. I can't tell you what to do, not like your pa, but I reckon he'd be mighty disappointed if you was to not get any more schooling. I can't tell you to learn, but I can tell you that there ain't no way I'm taking you and these goats to San Antone. You insist on going, then Shoelink and me is pulling our feet out of here."

Anger flashed in his eyes, then softened. "Okay, Gil. I'll do what you say."

I reached over and gently cuffed his ear. "That's a boy. Don't worry. Your time to push goats is coming. The way your pa planned, every two years, you and Mutt'll be taking two thousand or so goats to market."

He frowned and looked to the southeast. "I don't know if I could do it by myself or not." He looked up at me. "You'll be here, won't you?"

"No." I shook my head. "Like I told your pa, I got plans to buy me a ranch up in the Tetons." His forehead knit in disappointment. I explained. "A man wants a place of his own, Sam. Like you have here. Besides, you're growing faster'n a bad temper. You're almost a young man now. You can hire a good man to come in here and help."

My ears burned with guilt. I sounded a lot more positive than I felt, but I didn't want him to feel bad. At the same time, I had a life of my own, and I didn't want to be saddled down with a kid. I had a lot of living and working to do. I'd meet my obligation to him and his pa, then head out.

After the first of the year, we began laying plans for the drive. Wash had said it would take thirty days, but that was with him. I gave me and Shoelink an extra fifteen. With him leading the Judas goat, we could cover about ten miles a day.

San Antone was three hundred miles, as the crow flies. But we couldn't go in a straight line. That would have meant fording the Rio Grande twice, a dangerous undertaking I didn't even want to consider.

We could have used an extra hand, someone trustworthy to help us and bring Sam's profits back, but everyone in Hankering just laughed when I asked. I wanted to take Mutt, but I figured it would be a heap easier to talk Sam into staying if he could keep Mutt with him.

Finally, I had to settle for the fact that all I had was me and Shoelink, and that meant that after I sold the goats, I had to return to the ranch.

That was another setback. I wouldn't be able to hire on to a drive in San Antone, but I figured I could hurry back, then cut across country and pick up a herd at the Llano River in Mason County.

We rigged a small cart to hitch to Shoelink's burro for

our gear and grub, but after studying the contraption, decided to fashion aparejos instead. The two leather saddle packs would carry our grub, gear, and possibles.

I could lead the burro behind Ned, my roan.

We planned to leave in early March, but the does started dropping their newborn. Overnight, a new herd of tiny kids appeared, bouncing around like rubber balls. I shook my head and looked out over the prairie. "How long does this go on?"

At my side, Sam frowned and shrugged. "Till it's over, I reckon."

I pored over Wash's pamphlets, but nothing was said about birthing, so I figured goats were like beeves, they give birth in the spring. Maybe by the first of April, most of it would be over.

In the meantime, we had to decide which goats to take and which to leave behind as a replacement herd. "I reckon it's just like cows," I said to Shoelink and Sam. "We'll keep the ones that look like they can rebuild the herd."

And that's what we did, at least, as best we could. We moved almost five hundred into a box canyon we had fenced with saplings and ocotillo. The canyon was almost a mile square, with more than enough browse for the replacements until we could move out.

The day before Shoelink and me pulled out, Margaret and her pa came by to pick up Sam. We all rode out to the canyon to check on the replacement herd one more time. Margaret looked mighty fetching in her riding outfit, but she treated me like I had the mange.

I cleared my throat. "Sam. You and Mutt come over every day and check the herd. After we've been gone about a week, let 'em out. We'll be sixty or seventy miles from here. I don't reckon none of these will follow then."

He fought back the tears. "You sure I can't go with you, Gil? I won't cause no trouble."

"No." I shook my head. "Like I said, Sam, you need schooling. Miss Margaret here, she can learn you good." I glanced at Joshua Curtice. He gave me an understanding nod. I continued. "For your pa's sake, Sam, I want you to stay here and do everything she tells you, you hear? You and Mutt ride over from their place tomorrow morning and look after things. You hear?"

He snuffled once or twice, then nodded. "I hear." He scratched Mutt's ears.

I smiled at her. "I appreciate you and your pa looking after Sam, Miss Margaret."

Her smile was frosty. "Sam will be fine." She hesitated, glanced at Sam, and dropped her eyes. "Be careful . . . for Sam's sake," she hastily added.

"Don't worry. We oughta be back here in a couple months."

Chapter Seven

That night, I slept in snatches, constantly going back over all of our plans. We had water, and there were plenty of sweet water streams along the way. Packed in the aparejos was coffee, jerky, beans, and flour. Any other grub, Shoelink and me would have to find along the trail.

As much as I hated goats, I couldn't contain the excitement of moving out on a drive, even with goats. Finally, well before sunrise, I rose and put on the coffee.

I glanced out the bunkhouse window at the dark ranch house, and for a moment, felt a pang of disappointment that Sam wasn't around, but the good-byes yesterday had been tough enough. I didn't need them this morning.

After a hurried breakfast of biscuits and coffee, we put out the fire and rolled our soogans. Without a backward look, I blew out the lantern and closed the door behind me. It seemed strange not to see Mutt waiting at the threshold for me. I shrugged.

Shoelink tied the pack saddles on the burro while I saddled Ned. As false dawn lit the sky, I climbed aboard. "Well. You ready to move out?"

The diminutive Oriental nodded slowly. "Ai."

Just as the sun pushed its blood-red arch into the unclouded sky, Shoelink broke into his song and led out in his typical brisk walk, favoring his left leg and holding the tether for the Judas goat. And like well-mannered children, the other goats fell in behind.

I sat astride the roan for fifteen minutes before the last of the goats passed. We were strung out a mile, I guessed. Taking a deep breath, and not having an inkling of what we might run into, I fell in behind.

The first few days went smoothly. We lost a few goats to marauding wolves and coyotes, but generally, the goats remained close to the herd, and random slugs from my Winchester or side arm kept the predators spooked away. On the third day, we hit Coyanosa Draw, where we found enough water to replenish our supplies and give the goats their fill.

Travel was easy. The Stockton Plateau was covered with lush stands of creosote bush, tarbush, catclaw, whitethorn as well as yucca and juniper savannahs surrounded by tobosa and black grama flats. There were many poisonous plants, threadleaf goundsel, broom snakeweek, rayless goldenrod, but the goats seemed to know which to browse, and which to pass by.

Evening grub usually consisted of roasted rabbit, a couple biscuits, and strong coffee. Breakfast was leftovers and stronger coffee. Noon, we chewed on hard biscuits and jerky and washed them down with sweet water.

Quickly we got into a routine, up before dawn and on the trail before the sun, which put on a spectacular display every morning, rising all blood red and for a brief moment, turning the horizon to midnight black.

Midmorning of the third day, a curious noise echoed from our back trail. I slipped the Winchester from its sheath and scooted around in the saddle. The sound faded into the moan of the wind, only to intensify as the breeze dropped.

Suddenly, a dark object appeared in the middle of the

whitethorn and yucca, bouncing across the tobosa and black grama flats.

Wolves.

I threw the Winchester to my shoulder and squinted down the barrel. Just as my finger began to tighten on the trigger, I recognized the bouncing, awkward gait of the object. Mutt. Mutt was bobbing across the prairie on his three legs like a miniature kangaroo.

I swung off Ned as the red hound raced up. He leaped up and licked at my face, then rubbed against my leg. I scratched his ears roughly. "You old hound. What the blazes you doing out here?" I peered over the backtrail, half expecting to see Sam, but all I spotted was empty prairie.

"You old rascal." I knelt and hugged his neck. "I reckon Sam is mighty put out with you about now."

Mutt was even happy to see Shoelink, who whipped up extra beans and biscuits for the hound. Animals seemed to gravitate toward the diminutive Oriental.

Shoelink had a special rapport with the bell goat, an old doe who was the recognized queen of the herd. The second morning out, just before sunrise, the old doe had pushed her way through the herd and come to stand beside our camp, dutifully awaiting the sash about her neck.

The same the third morning.

By the fourth morning, my curiosity got the best of me. I shook my head at Shoelink and gestured to the goat. "How?"

He frowned.

I fell back on my sign language, which was just as garbled as my conversation with him. I pointed to him and then the goat. "Why she come here every morning?" I gestured to the campfire and then the sun.

He nodded emphatically. "Ahhh. Yes. Zhou Gui

Ling...." He touched his chest, then pointed to the doe. "The goat are together." He placed his palms, one over the other, on his chest. Then he tapped his head. "We are one."

All I could do was stare at him. "What do you mean, you are one? You think as one? That's a goat there, not a person."

He frowned at me, cocked his head, and wrinkled his brow. He didn't understand a word I was saying. Wearily, I shook my head and grinned at him. "Forget it. You're doing good." I nodded emphatically.

His eyes twinkled, and a tiny grin played over his lips. "You like? *Sangsu* like much?"

"Yeah, you little sawed-off squirt. I like much." We both laughed.

To the north a few days later, Panther Mesa and Pine Mesa loomed along our trail, like somber sentinels overlooking our journey. Wolves flanked the herd at a distance, kept there by Mutt's constant barking and occasional shots from my Winchester.

I'd learned as a younker that you spooked animals by knocking up dust or rocks around them, not by killing them. If one wolf in a pack falls, they pay little attention, but let a slug knock up a chunk of soil and go whining past, they'll scatter.

On the few cattle drives I'd punched over the past few years, as soon as my head hit my blankets at night, I was asleep. To my surprise, goat herding was easier. After all, I just tagged along, leading the burro loaded down with pack saddles. What few goats strayed, returned quickly, never venturing more than a hundred yards from the main body of the herd.

By the end of the first week, I had a new respect for

Washington Cottle, and for his goats. The man knew what he was doing. A blasted shame he went out and got himself killed.

About the time I started relaxing, the first band of riders hit, just after noon on the seventh day.

We had reached the edge of the caprock and stood on a ridge of red sandstone. Below, the black grama gave way to hairy grama and bluestem, along with thick stands of buffalo grass and witchgrass, for the soil was thinning, and the goats were moving at a fair pace. Ahead were thick forests of scrub oak and juniper, dotted with patches of mesquite. Behind, the prairie lay flat and empty.

The riders struck from the scrub oak below, and slashed through the middle of the herd, screaming like wild men and blazing away at the frightened animals.

I yanked my Winchester from the sheath and began firing, but between my roan dancing around and the riders moving so fast, my shots went wild. The burro spun away, ripping the lead rope from my hand.

By the time I settled my own pony down, the riders were a quarter of a mile away, disappearing over a rise. To my surprise, only two animals were killed, but our herd had scattered across the prairie and down into the scrub.

I reined Ned up tight and cursed. I glared at the cloud of dust disappearing in the distance. Blake. Mike Blake. But why? Because of Shoelink? That didn't make sense. Blake had to know that both Shoelink and me were leaving the state after this drive.

While I sat staring after the riders, Shoelink approached, leading the bell goat. He looked up at me. "*Sangsu* hurt?"

I growled. "No. Mad, but not hurt." I gestured to the scattered goats around us. They were spread from the forest below to as far as the eye could see across the prairie. ''It'll take us all day to gather them.''

Shoelink shook his head and a faint smile curled his lips. Whistling softly, he led the bell goat onto the prairie. I couldn't believe my eyes. The goats within hearing of his whistle drifted toward him. The goats beyond sound of his whistling saw the other goats moving to him, so they followed.

In his leisurely pace, Shoelink headed back across the prairie until he was almost out of sight, then he began making a sweeping circle, making sure he passed within sound of the patches of scrub. By the time he returned, almost two hours later, three-quarters of the herd had rejoined him and the bell goat.

He paused by me on the ridge and nodded to the forest below. ''The others, we find there,'' he said matter-of-factly. ''Soon, they come to others.''

We camped at the base of the ridge on the edge of the scrub oak forest. Throughout the night, the herd called in its lost with a pitiful bleating. From every direction, goats ambled in all night. The next morning it appeared we had our herd back. I had no idea how many had been lost, but when they strung out after Shoelink that next morning for the last leg to the upper reaches of Big Canyon, there didn't seem to be any noticeable decrease in the size of the herd.

Before we broke camp, I made sure the Winchester and my .44 were loaded. All night, I tried to come up with some sensible reason Mike Blake would have for venturing out sixty or seventy miles, and not one explanation I came up with made sense.

Blake was brazen, bullying, bawling, and belligerent, but he wasn't stupid. He might pull a lot of foolish stunts, but a hundred-forty-mile ride just to prove his dislike for

Shoelink or as revenge for the ambush at Wild Rose Pass just didn't seem likely.

No. I couldn't make myself believe Blake was behind the attack.

And if Blake wasn't the source, then who in the blazes was? If the attack was more than merely an harassment, why didn't they make a second and third pass? Why only one?

I was stumped, but that didn't mean I wouldn't be ready. If the raiders hit again, they'd have their hands full. Shoelink watched apprehensively as I checked and double-checked my hardware. I grinned at him and slipped my side arm back in the holster. "No more bad men," I said, shaking my head and pointing in the direction the riders had taken.

"Ahhh. So." He nodded emphatically, and his eyes lit up. "Zhou Gui Ling understand *Sangsu*. No more bad men." He held out his hand, thumb up, forefinger extended, miming a six-gun. "Boom, boom. Bad men leave. Boom, boom, boom."

I couldn't help laughing. My little Chinese friend was becoming a regular chatterbox.

The scrub oak forest in which we camped that night gave way to grassy savannahs by early morning. For the next several hours, we tramped through a lush prairie of grass, stomach high to the goats. Midafternoon, we hit rocky soil and thinning grass. Creek bottoms were dry. Dust clogged our nostrils.

We reached Big Canyon Draw late. There were a few pools of water, so we bedded the herd around them. After a spare meal of beans and coffee, I left Shoelink in camp and made my way back to the rim, where I snuggled down in a patch of ashe juniper near the edge. If we had unwelcome visitors tonight, I wanted to give them a greeting they wouldn't forget.

An old moon illumined the countryside with a cold, blue light, striking the juniper and mesquite in stark relief against the prairie. A chill rolled in. I buttoned my vest and pulled a blanket around my shoulders. In the distance, coyotes wailed. From time to time, the squeal of a frightened rabbit echoed through the darkness.

My eyes burned, and my lids grew heavy. I leaned my head back against the rough bark of the juniper and closed my eyes.

Suddenly, I jerked awake. I had no idea how long I had dozed, but the shadows in which I hunkered had moved, leaving me in the middle of the moonlight. I blinked and cursed, trying to shake the sleep from my eyes.

On the trail, I was a light sleeper, my subconscious always alert for any disturbance out of the ordinary. Something had awakened me, something out of the ordinary, something that didn't belong. I squinted into the darkness and strained my ears.

The light breeze rustled the oak leaves like the faint riffling of a deck of poker cards. Occasional cries from night birds, and the distant wail of coyotes was all I heard. Those were sounds common to the prairie at night. Something else had awakened me.

I tightened my grip on the Winchester.

Then I heard the sound again, the light clatter of hooves against rocks. I narrowed my eyes, trying to penetrate the darkness. The sound drifted in and out of my hearing as the thin breeze ebbed and flowed, but one thing was certain, it was growing closer.

I touched my tongue to my dry lips and leaned forward so I could grasp the trunk of a juniper with my left hand.

I rested the forearm of the Winchester on my hand and sighted along the barrel.

My mind raced. Only one, maybe two riders approaching. Who were they? Blake? No. The riders from two days earlier? Perhaps. Drifters? Unlikely. If they were drifters, why weren't they camped? Why move at night? Unless the law was after them. Or unless they wanted to take over the herd, which at one time I would have thought ridiculous, but realizing the several thousand dollars the goats would bring, such a move would be worth the risk. Back in Hankering, everyone knew about the drive. Maybe a cowpoke or two decided to pick up some easy money. My body began to throb from tension.

Taking a deep breath, I forced my muscles to relax. The sounds grew more pronounced, and finally, I was convinced that it was only one rider.

In the distance, a dark shadow appeared against the blue background of the moonlit prairie. I caught my breath. "There you are," I whispered, shifting around so I could hold the butt of the Winchester in my shoulder more comfortably. "Just keep coming."

Abruptly, the horse whinnied. A voice yelled, then grew silent. After a moment, the animal started moving once again.

I leaned forward, straining to make out the shadow. The click of hooves on rock grew clearer, and gradually, the fuzzy silhouette of the horse and rider grew into sharper focus.

My breath came faster. I tightened my finger on the trigger. Whoever the jasper was, he had some tall explaining to do.

The dark shadow grew larger until finally I guessed it was less than thirty feet away.

"Hold on, right there, stranger," I said, my voice harsh

and cold. "I got a .44 Winchester aimed at your chest. One move, and you'll buy a six-foot-deep hole."

The horse jerked to a halt.

A thin, frightened voice broke the silence. "Gil?"

My jaw dropped to the toes of my boots. "Sam? Sampson Cottle? Is that you?"

Chapter Eight

Shoelink and I sat around the campfire watching as young Sam wolfed down the remainder of the beans and choked down the last of the biscuits. He got the hiccups and had to wash it all down with several large gulps of water. I had a hundred questions, but I knew I wouldn't get any straight answers until his belly was full.

I unbuttoned my vest. Down in the draw, we were protected from the breeze. The heat of the fire bouncing off the rocky walls on either side warmed us. Mutt sat motionless, staring at Sam. From time to time, his ears stiffened as night sounds drifted into camp. One or twice, he darted from the firelight, and we could hear frenzied barking for several seconds before it died out. Moments later, he returned to camp and took his place, his eyes on Sam.

Finally, Sam drew his hand across his mouth.

"Okay, boy," I said. "Now tell us what's going on. What the blazes you doing out here? Something happen back at the Curtices'?"

Sam unbuttoned his mackinaw and glanced at Shoelink sheepishly. He hung his head. "No, Sir. Everything was fine. Mr. Curtice and Miss Margaret, they was real good to me."

I eyed him narrowly. "Then what prompted you to come out here?"

He hesitated. His cheeks, weathered brown, blushed. He nodded at Mutt. ''I came to see if Mutt was all right.''

''Don't hand me that.'' I eyed him skeptically.

''But he was gone, Gil. I was worried about him.'' Sam looked to Shoelink for support.

''Ah, yes. Young master worry over animal. Zhou Gui Ling understand.''

Without warning, Mutt barked and raced into the darkness, yapping incessantly. Coyotes, I figured, pushing it from my mind, for I suddenly realized Shoelink and Sam had me outnumbered. ''I understand too, but I don't care about the hound. You've gone and caused Miss Margaret and her pa a lot of worry.'' I shook my head. No way I could take him back. Here we were, some eighty miles from the ranch. A three-day round-trip. And what would Shoelink do with the herd? What would happen if the riders decided to hit while I was gone?

I clenched my teeth and glared at the boy. He had created me a mighty big problem.

Shoelink and Sam watched me expectantly. I cursed under my breath. I was whipped. And I was mad. The entire situation was being jammed down my throat, and I didn't like it one little bit.

I had no choice. ''Listen to me, Sam, and listen good. I can't take you back, so you're stuck here with us.''

His eyes lit up and a broad grin split his face.

''But that doesn't mean I like it, or what you did was right,'' I added, wiping the grin from his face. ''You were wrong. Your pa wouldn't like it, you putting yourself in all kinds of danger by coming out here like you did.''

He dropped his eyes to the ground.

For a moment, I felt guilty about jumping him, but then I realized that had the boy's pa been here, Sam would have caught the spanking of his life. So, my scolding the boy was probably a good thing. "When did you leave?" I asked.

"Three days ago," he replied in a thin, penitent voice. "I took some food and a canteen of water."

I thought back as to when Mutt showed up. I shook my head and poured some more coffee, suppressing a smile. After the hound left, that probably set Sam to thinking. Now all I needed was for Margaret to show up. I decided to make Sam feel as bad as I could before we hit the sack. "How do you think Miss Margaret and her pa are feeling about now? I reckon you've got them worried sick. They're fine, fine folks, and they don't deserve to be treated the way you treated them."

His bottom lip quivered, and his eyes glistened with tears in the firelight. "I . . . I, ah . . ."

I tossed my coffee on the fire. Sparks flews and coals hissed. "Forget it," I growled. "Get to bed."

Sam stammered out an apology. "I . . . I'm sorry, Gil. I just wanted to be out here with you and Shoe. . . ."

I waved his words away angrily, though I wasn't nearly as perturbed as I let on to the boy. "I don't want to hear no more about it. You just get to bed and think about the worry and pain you're causing Miss Margaret. I reckon they're at their wits' end by now."

A sharp voice cut through the darkness behind me. "Why don't you ask her and see."

I stared at Shoelink, my eyes bulging. I knew that voice. Lord sakes alive, how I knew that voice.

Finally, I shook myself from my stupor and spun.

In the bend of the draw a few yards distant, Margaret Curtice was frowning down at us from her pinto pony.

I rolled my eyes. What else could go wrong?

* * *

Around the fire, Margaret brought us up to date. After Sam disappeared, she followed. "Pa wanted to come, but he couldn't. He's sick with influenza."

I frowned. "Influenza could be a killer. Maybe you should've stayed with him. He might be needing you."

"No." She sipped her coffee. "Snag. He's our cook. He's better than any doctor. No, Pa's in good hands. Snag's swabbing his throat with coal oil and got his chest covered with camphor poultices."

I winced at the remedies. Western doctoring sometimes handed out cures worse than the illnesses.

She saw me grimace and quickly added. "Oh, Snag's giving him black cat tail tea for the fever. So there's no need for me to be there."

"At least, not . . . just right away, huh?" I crossed my fingers, hoping a stroke of luck would fall in my lap with a solution as to how I could get them safely back to the Circle W without bringing the drive to a halt.

"Oh, there's no rush," she replied lightly. "Tomorrow will be fine." She patted the six-gun on her hip. "Who knows, we might ride along with you for a day or so."

By now I was in a real quandary. Only a fool would continue the drive with a child and a woman, yet I couldn't turn around and go back. And I couldn't send them back by themselves, not as long as that band of owlhoots was still out there.

I sighed wearily, unable to dredge up any solution except to keep them with the drive, and hope for the best. Suddenly, I remembered the goats back at the ranch.

"Don't worry," Margaret said when I asked who was looking after them. "Pa ordered two of our hands to look after them. You don't have to worry. After all, the boys Pa sent are good cattle men. All you have is goats."

For several seconds, I stared at her, dumbfounded. Then,

without a word, I nodded and lay back on my saddle. What I needed now was sleep.

I didn't sleep much that night. My nerves were scraped raw with worry.

And the next morning around the breakfast campfire didn't help.

Margaret insisted on taking Sam and Mutt back that morning. "I didn't see any sign of outlaws. Besides, I got to thinking about what you said last night, about Pa needing me, so I decided to head back this morning. We got water, and you can spare some grub . . . beans and coffee. Besides, I have my six-gun. We'll feast on rabbit." She insisted.

I glanced at Shoelink, then cleared my throat. "There's something I didn't tell you."

She frowned. "Like what?"

"Night riders." Quickly, I related the details of the raid on our herd at the draw. "And that's why I can't let you two go back by yourselves."

Margaret studied me for several seconds. Her tone was edged with a hint of scorn. "There's no question what you say happened, did actually take place . . . I mean about the riders, but even you admit you haven't seen them in several days. Chances are, it was a bunch of drunken cowhands heading home and thought they would hurrah the goats for a little fun."

To be honest, her explanation could be the answer. I didn't think so, but then I knew there was no way I could convince her to stay. And I couldn't let them go back by themselves. I didn't have a choice. Shoelink would have to hold the herd here until I returned.

"I won't argue the point, Miss Margaret. And if you want to take the boy and hound back, that's fine. I'll take you. But you and I both know, the only way you can keep

Mutt back at the ranch is to tie him up, and first chance he got, he'd be back here.''

She sipped her coffee thoughtfully. ''I suppose you're right, Mr. Vince.'' She looked at Sam. ''In that case, we'll leave Mutt here. He can help with the goats.''

Sam looked at me hopefully. ''Please, Gil. Can't I stay with you and Shoelink? I promise . . .''

The racketing of gunfire broke the predawn stillness. Wild cries echoed across the savannah, and a dozen wild-riding cowpokes raced around a bend in the arroyo and headed straight through the herd, firing point-blank at the animals. One swerved toward us, raising his handgun. He hesitated, then fired into the air above our heads and galloped away.

I shoved Margaret and Sam to the ground. In the same motion, I grabbed my Winchester and clanked a shell into the chamber. The riders had come up the draw and were pushing the goats ahead of them.

I dropped to one knee and fired rapidly. In the melee of goats and riders, one horse reared and fell backward, throwing its rider, who instantly jumped to his feet and with the help of one of his *compadres*, swung up behind the saddle and the two of them disappeared into the night.

Thirty seconds later, they were gone, leaving behind several dead goats. I jumped to my feet and shook the Winchester after the riders, then turned back to Margaret. ''You still think we're dealing with a band of drunk cowboys?''

Without giving her time to respond, I stalked up the draw to the dead horse. My slug had whipped past the rider's shoulder when the horse reared and struck the unlucky animal behind the ears and exited its forehead. ''Blast,'' I muttered. Seemed like the innocent were always the ones hurt. I hated the fate of the animal, but at least it was fast. He didn't suffer.

I studied the rigging, and then my eyes fastened on the brand on the pony's rump. My heart thudded against my chest. "What the. . . ."

Margaret heard my exclamation. "What's wrong?"

"See for yourself." My eyes burned into the brand, the Slash Bar, John Howard's brand.

Behind me, feet crunched in the sand. "What is it?"

"That." I pointed to the brand. "Recognize it?"

For a moment, she remained silent. When she spoke, her voice was strained. "Why, that's . . . that's . . ."

"Yeah." I finished the sentence for her. "That's John Howard's brand."

Chapter Nine

Standing on the rim of Big Canyon Draw, I muttered a curse at my own stupidity for camping down in the dry bed. Even a tenderfoot should have known to make a camp where he could keep an eye on the surrounding terrain. Yet, something puzzled me.

The cowpoke who had swerved toward us—why did he hesitate? Why did he shoot into the air? Just to scare us? I grimaced, confused. If I was going to take a herd, I'd take it. Get rid of the owners and take it.

Margaret and Sam sat astride their ponies, silently watching while I snugged down the aparejos on the burro. Shoelink had already moved out with the remainder of the herd, heading east toward the Pecos River without bothering to gather the animals that had run from the riders. From experience, we knew that the goats hadn't scattered like sheep or beeves, but instead had run only a few hundred yards before darting aside and hiding in the underbrush.

When I swung into the saddle, Margaret spoke up, her voice chilly. "I still can't believe John Howard is behind this. Why, his place is twice the size of Sam's and ours together."

I slammed the Winchester in its boot. "Greed does strange things, Miss Margaret."

She tugged her sand-colored hat down over her eyes.

"Well, just the same, Sam and I are going back. If John Howard is behind this, he won't hurt us."

I stared at her in disbelief. She must've been behind the door when the good Lord passed out common sense. "Look, Miss Curtice, like it or not, you and Sam are staying here with us, with the herd. There's no way I'm letting you two pull foot out of here, and I can't take a chance on Shoelink holding the herd here for three or four days. Howard's riders could come back. Even if they don't, these goats will clean up the browse in an all-fired hurry and insist on moving out. Unless we keep them directed, they'll end up drifting all over this part of Texas."

She glared at me. "You can't tell me what to do."

Sam looked at me hopefully, then back at her. He was uncomfortable, caught in the middle like he was.

"I am telling you, and if you give me any trouble, I'll hog-tie you to that pinto like a sack of corn."

Margaret Curtice gave me a look that was as savage as a meat axe. For several seconds, she glowered at me. I could see her mind working.

I hoped she wouldn't push the matter. I didn't want to get rough with her, but I couldn't let her or the boy ride out. There was a hundred miles of danger behind us. Just because she was too blind to see the peril didn't let me off the hook.

Then I had an idea. "Tell you what. You and Sam come along with us. If we run across some freight wagons or an army patrol, you can go back with them."

Margaret arched an eyebrow. Her eyes blazed. I had the sick feeling that she was going to buck me, but then her face softened, and she relaxed. "All right, Mr. Vince. If you feel that strongly about it, we'll stay, but only until someone comes along who we can travel with."

I grinned at Sam, then dipped my head to her. "Yes, Ma'am."

By now, the last of the goats had fallen into line, and we dropped in behind them. The country grew rougher, split by ravines and dry creek beds, choked with juniper and mesquite, all held together by long slender grapevines that hung from trees and draped over bushes like popcorn strings on a Christmas tree.

Shoelink kept moving east, leading the bell goat, weaving through the thick brush and over the rocky terrain.

Margaret and Sam trailed behind me, from time to time dropping out of sight when we skirted a patch of juniper or dipped down into a creek bed.

I relaxed, at least, as much as I could. Any time a jasper pushed animals anywhere, he had his hands full, but throw a headstrong woman and a child into the mix, and he'll find himself with a sticky concoction more dangerous than standing on a block of ice while balancing a vial of nitroglycerin on his forehead.

Once, I reined up, looking over our back trail, waiting for Margaret and Sam. Finally, they appeared from behind a swath of juniper. I urged my pony on after the herd.

The sun burned down from a clear sky. Sweat rolled down my back. Midmorning, a breeze rose from the southwest, drying the perspiration on my face and blowing the trail dust aside.

Once, I thought I heard a shout, but when I looked around, I saw nothing amiss. Margaret and Sam were still out of sight behind the last sandstone ridge we'd skirted. I shrugged and patted my roan's neck. "Out of sight, out of mind, ain't that right, feller?" I chuckled at my own feeble wit.

The breeze stiffened.

Clouds built back to the southwest, rising into towering

pinnacles. Without warning, the herd slowed and began to bunch. "Hey, hey, hey," I shouted, waving my hat in an effort to keep them moving, but they were determined to stay where they were.

Every time I approached, they turned to face me, even the tiny kids lowering their heads threateningly. "You blasted, worthless pieces of contrary. . . ." Suddenly, I realized the reason for their behavior.

I scooted around in my saddle and stared back to the southwest. Sure enough, a bank of black clouds rolled forward, spitting out lightning and snorting thunder. "I should've guessed," I muttered, glancing over my shoulder.

Margaret and Sam were nowhere in sight. I reined my pony around, but Shoelink stopped me. "*Sangsu*. Storm come." He nodded to the rapidly approaching clouds and pointed to a small canyon choked with wrist-sized shin oak and redberry juniper. "Cave. We go there." Mutt was at his heels.

I squinted back into the canyon, but I couldn't see any cave.

He looked down our back trail. "Where boy and Missy Margaret?" He gestured emphatically to the approaching weather and then the cave. "Bad, bad storm. Must go to cave." He waved me toward the cave.

"No." I shook my head and pointed down the backtrail. "You go to cave. I find Margaret and boy." I saw the defiance in his eyes. "You stay with goats. I find Margaret and boy. Yes?"

Shoelink considered my suggestion. Without a word, he took the lead rope for the burro and scurried back into the canyon. I grinned after him, but then I remembered Margaret and Sam, and the smile turned into a frown.

"What the Sam Hill is keeping them? They should be here by now."

With a click of my tongue, I sent the roan jittering back down the trail, cursing under my breath, expecting to run into them around the sandstone ridge. But to my surprise, there was no sign of them on the trail.

"What the dickens?" I grumbled and reined up, staring around me in the underbrush and patches of juniper. Were they playing some kind of trick on us? A lopsided grin played over my face. Maybe they just got bored and figured on a joke to pass the time, but even as I considered the ridiculous idea, I knew something more had taken place.

I studied the ground. In the midst of the goat signs, I found my pony's tracks along with those of the burro, but nowhere did I find Sam and Margaret's. Slowly, I worked back down the trial. A quarter of a mile back, I discovered where they had turned and headed back in the direction from which we had come.

For the life of me, I couldn't understand what was going on. The sign was easy to read, but the explanation was what I couldn't figure. They had stopped. Their ponies had stomped around, then the shoes cut deeper into the thin soil as the two animals bolted back down the trail, one after the other.

Shucking my six-gun, I spurred Ned into a trot back along the trail, puzzling over the sign. My first thought was John Howard and his bunch, but there were no tracks following the two sets. Whatever had happened, Margaret and Sam weren't being pursued, yet the stride of their ponies made it plain they were galloping.

Suddenly, an idea hit me, but I immediately dismissed the thought, considering the notion too far-fetched. But the longer I trailed them, the longer I studied the sign, the more I began to wonder.

The right-hand tracks of the lead pony cut deeper into the thin soil, suggesting a shift of weight to that side of the horse. Why? Shifting in the saddle was a common means to ease the pounding of miles of travel, but not at a gallop, and that was exactly what the animals' stride suggested.

I shook my head. The only logical explanation had to be that the front rider was leading the trailing animal. That would account for the shift in position in the saddle. But why?

The wind continued stiffening. Thunder growled across the rugged countryside, and lightning cracked in the distance. Moments later, I topped out on a ridge and jerked my roan to a halt. A surge of anger burned my ears.

Half a mile distant, Margaret Curtice raced through the middle of a yucca savannah, leading Sam's pony while he clutched the saddle horn with both hands. His hat bounced up and down on his back, held by the tie cord around his throat.

I clenched my teeth. Of all the empty-headed, lockjawed stunts, this one had to be the biggest toad in the puddle. That woman had to be addle-brained to think she could get both her and Sam over a hundred miles of prairie and scrub forests to the Circle W with only two canteens of water and the six-gun on her hip.

In the distance, a gray wall of rain blocked out the scrub forest and prairie beyond. Like a freight train, the rain burst on the savannah and instantly engulfed Margaret and Sam. Just before they vanished from sight, Margaret's pony cut to the side and reared, sending her tumbling backward to the ground.

I cried out to my pony. "Come on, fella." I dug my spurs into Ned's flanks and sent him down the steep ridge. At the same time, I jerked my poncho over my head. Seconds later, the rain blinded me, but my roan was surefooted.

He twisted his way down the slope and onto the savannah. I kept my head ducked into the storm.

The first blast of rain swept past. From the downpour ahead, I heard shouts. I peered into the storm. "Come on, Ned," I shouted, leaning over the roan's neck. "They're just ahead."

Unerringly, the pony took me directly to Margaret and Sam. She was on her feet, trying to steady her horse so she could mount, but the rain had the animal spooked, and he refused to stand still.

Sam's pony jittered around, the reins dragging in the mud, which I grabbed and tossed to the boy. Then I moved Ned up beside her pony so the frightened animal couldn't back away as she mounted.

When she swung into the saddle, I leaned forward and yelled. "Follow me."

She looked up at me from under the wide brim of her hat. Rain drilled her face. I could see the fear in her eyes. She nodded, and I headed back to the cave. Overhead, thunder boomed from the black clouds, and lightning cut dazzling slashes through the heavens.

The canyon was packed with goats trying to stay out of the weather. We pushed through the herd and the wet underbrush to the cave. Several critters stood forlornly in the mouth of the cave, prevented from moving any farther inside by the fire Shoelink had built beyond the reach of the storm.

Behind the fire, the cave opened into a large chamber room where we unsaddled our ponies and laid out our rigs to dry. The rich aroma of coffee filled the cave, smothering even the wet stink of the goats.

Eagerly, Margaret and Sam huddled by the fire, holding out their hands and turning their backs to the blaze in an effort to warm up and dry out. A pot of beans bubbled and a pan of biscuits baked on the coals. Mutt lay stretched on the ground in front of the fire.

I shed my poncho and squatted across the fire. "You ought to shed those duds and let 'em dry," I said, pouring a cup of coffee and offering it to her.

Margaret held the cup in both hands and nodded. "I prefer the coffee, if you don't mind."

"Do what you want. Fine with me." I poured another cup and looked up at Sam. "Wrap yourself in a blanket, boy. Let's let those clothes dry."

He glanced at Margaret.

I chuckled. "Nobody's going to look. Get back there in the dark."

A blush colored Sam's cheeks, but he quickly disappeared back into the cave and returned moments later wrapped in a blanket and carrying his wet clothes, which he draped over a large boulder near the fire.

Margaret remained standing, water from her clothes forming a puddle at her feet. I kept quiet. That she had a mind of her own was obvious. No one was going to push her into anything she didn't want, so I just leaned back and enjoyed my coffee, and her misery in those soaking wet duds.

Unless she got them dried out, come early morning, she'd come down with a case of the shivers that would rattle her teeth. But, she had a mind of her own. Far be it from me to interfere.

"One thing, I'd like to know," I said later as we sat around the fire eating our beans and biscuits. "Why did you and Sam run away like that? It's over a hundred miles back to the Circle W."

Margaret, who perched on a small boulder next to the cave wall, glared at me. "So?"

"So, I'm not trying to tell you what to do. You're a grown woman. You can do what you want, but I just don't understand what possessed you to run away like you did."

"I can take care of us."

I chuckled. "Yeah. I saw an example of that."

Her eyes blazed. "I would have gotten on the horse, and I could have found us some place to take shelter in. I didn't need *you* to butt in."

Sam kept his head down and shoveled beans as fast as he could.

"All right. I'll concede. You could take care of yourself, but just tell me why you would want to cover a hundred miles of prairie when you know blasted well there's a band of rustlers out there trying to take over the herd."

"You don't know that for sure," she shot back. "If they were, why haven't they come back?" She sniffed. "Personally, I don't think they want the herd if all they do is ride through here and hurrah everyone."

As much as I hated to admit it, she had touched on a theory I had tossed about myself, one that I hadn't been able to answer. "That's not the point. All I'm saying is that you don't need to run off again. You want to go back, I'll take you. Just wait until we can find a spot with enough browse to take care of the herd for three or four days. Okay?"

She eyed me suspiciously. Finally she nodded. "Okay."

I glanced at Sam, who was still bent over his plate. I knew he had heard every word, and I knew he wanted to continue the drive, but I also knew that Margaret Curtice was so hardheaded that she would insist he return with her, if for no other reason than to spite me.

Chapter Ten

During the night, the fire died, and a chill invaded the cave along with the rank stench of the wet goats. I awakened to hear Margaret chattering. I was sorely tempted to stay between my nice, warm blankets and let her suffer, but I also realized that if she became ill, we'd have to pull up until she was well.

With a grim smile, I rose and stoked the fire, building it back into a blaze. I glanced at her. To my surprise, she was watching me. Her teeth continued to chatter. After the fire was blazing, I shook out one of my blankets and spread it over her. "I was getting up anyway," I said, lying.

She smiled and closed her eyes. Moments later, with the fire blazing and another blanket to hold in the warmth, she closed her eyes and dozed.

Outside, the rain continued, though not as heavy as the night before. I had the feeling we were in for a spell of weather. I squatted by the fire and put on the coffee, listening to the steady patter of the rain on the leaves outside.

More than once, I had holed up in caves during storms, staying snug and dry while the elements outside raged.

An hour later, the sun rose, but the rain continued.

Midmorning, I ventured out, concerned that we might be sitting right in the path of a flood, but to my relief, our cave was twenty feet above the adjoining canyon floor, well beyond reach of a flash flood.

"Why are we just sitting here?" Margaret frowned when I returned. "The rain isn't going to hurt the goats or us."

Shoelink smiled and clucked his tongue. "Goats not like rain, Missy. Goats not move. Not like much."

I chuckled. "He's right. I found out the hard way with those knuckleheads out there. They hate rain. Once they get situated in a storm, they're there until it's over."

Sam stood in the mouth of the cave, staring above the backs of the goats at the rugged hills surrounding us, dark green peaks washed shiny by the rain. "It sure is pretty out here, Gil."

Margaret just sniffed and turned back to the fire.

"Yeah. I reckon it is, boy." I stopped beside Sam and stared out over the hills and canyons spreading before us, miles of rugged country, unfriendly, unforgiving, but beautiful.

"Tell you what," I said, reaching for my Winchester. "How about you and me seeing if we can bring some meat in here?" I squinted at the gray skies. "Looks like we might be here a couple more days.

Margaret cleared her throat. "Hunting? I don't know. Sam is just a boy."

I brushed her concerns aside. "That's when he needs to go. I guarantee you, this is something he'll never forget, even if we don't find anything."

She frowned. I should have known she wouldn't understand, but that was no matter. Sam understood. The mile-wide grin on his face testified to that.

We donned ponchos and eased out into the rain with Mutt at our heels. I yelled at the animal, and he skulked back into the cave.

Sam whispered. "Where do you suppose we'll find them, Gil?"

I whispered back. "Bedded down, likely." I pointed down the canyon. "We'll just pussyfoot down this way, then ease up the side of the hill yonder," I said, gesturing to a peak rising several hundred feet above us.

Sneaking Injun-like through the scrub oak forest brought back memories of when I was a kid and hunted for game before Pa died. Then, the pursuit was fun, but after he passed on, the hunt became serious. No game, no grub. When your next meal depends on your aim, you get mighty serious, mighty fast.

Luckily, the leaves were wet, so Sam's stumbling feet didn't disturb any game. Had the leaves been dry, the noise he made could have spooked everything for a mile around.

At the junction of our canyon with two others, I spotted deer signs in the dry soil beneath a ledge, under which the rain couldn't reach. I pointed them out to Sam. "Here's a trail, boy. See?"

The tracks led to a trail that wound up the mountain slope. "Look." A few hairs clung to a broken branch. Farther up the trail, we found fresh tracks still filling with water.

I glanced around. "Okay, Sam. Here's where we wait. Over there." I led the way into a small patch of juniper covered with wild grapevines, where we could squat and keep an eye on the trail. "Make yourself comfortable, boy. We might be here for a spell."

We both settled down. I had already made up my mind, Sam would get the shot. "Scoot on up here," I whispered.

He frowned.

I explained. "You want to shoot a deer, don't you?"

His eyes bugged out. I held my finger to my lips. "Quiet," I whispered. "Now scoot up here."

"All right, now. Sooner or later, a deer's going to pass by out there. You prop the barrel of the Winchester on one of those limbs and sight in just behind the animal's front leg. You hear?"

He nodded enthusiastically, his eyes shining, his face beaming. "I hear. I hear."

So we sat, cross-legged in our ponchos with the rain beating down on us. We were dry and snug. Minutes passed. From where we sat, we had a view of the countryside around us. Like Sam had said earlier, the country was mighty pretty.

Suddenly, Sam stiffened. I blinked.

Fifty yards distant, broadside to us, stood a deer.

I glanced at Sam. His hands were shaking. Suppressing my grin, I whispered. "Take a deep breath. Now, aim where I told you, then squeeze the trigger. Don't jerk."

Despite his nervousness, Sam followed my instructions.

Seconds later, the gunshot echoed across the hills and down the canyons. Sam leaped to his feet. "I got 'im. I got 'im. I got 'im."

I chuckled and hugged him to me. "You sure did, son. You sure did."

Shoelink whipped up a delicious pot of venison stew that evening, thickening the gravy with the potatolike bulbs from the plantain herbs he dug at the edge of a nearby pond. As the night fell, we slid between our blankets with full stomachs. Out of habit, I reached for my Bull Durham, finding instead only an empty pocket. "Oh, well," I muttered to myself, turning on my side and pulling the blanket up around my neck.

Outside, the rain seemed to be letting up. I dropped off to sleep hoping we could push out the next day.

I awakened during the night and for a moment lay staring

into the darkness above my head. Something had awakened me. I turned my head and stared out the mouth of the cave. In the distance, stars twinkled.

With a grin, I quickly rose and went outside. The rain had stopped. The last of the storm clouds, ripe with thunder and lightning, moved past the northeastern horizon. Back to the north, I found the Big Dipper. About midnight.

Back inside, I replenished the fire and returned to my blankets. I figured on rising about four and moving out before dawn. We had two days to make up.

Upon rising, I saddled and picketed the horses and the burro outside near some head-high browse the goats had been unable to reach. When I returned to the cave, Shoelink had coffee and biscuits on. Margaret and Sam had crawled from their blankets, which I rolled and packed away in the aparejos on the burro's back. Mutt followed me outside, spotted a rabbit, and like a kangaroo, bounced off through the underbrush after it.

Before I squatted for coffee, I had all the gear packed except the coffeepot and our breakfast utensils. "Get a move on, Shoelink. We're wasting daylight."

He looked at me, then cut his eyes to the predawn shadows beyond the mouth of the cave. With a brief nod, he turned back to the biscuits.

Sam grinned up at me. "Some of that stew would sure have tasted good this morning, huh, Gil?"

"Yeah." I winked at him. "I figured after last night, you wouldn't be hungry for a week."

He patted his stomach. "I'm starving."

"Well, if you be right nice, maybe Shoelink will whip up some more tonight. The rest of the venison is tied on the burro. We're going to be sick of venison before we finish with it, because we're sure not going to let it go to waste.''

''We could just get another one.''

I grew serious. ''No, boy. You don't waste like that. I don't like killing any animal, but some are put here to feed us, so when we take one, we use it all the way. Like the Injuns. They use every piece of the animal, down to the bones and sinews. When you do that, then you can justify killing, because it keeps you alive.'' Suddenly, an ear-shattering blast exploded the stillness of the early morning. The ground shuddered under our feet.

Margaret looked up at me, fear in her eyes.

Then I heard the rumble of boulders and rocks, and the roof of the cave began crumbling. Before I could move, a house-sized boulder dropped from the ceiling and sealed the mouth of the cave. ''Back,'' I yelled, shoving the three of them deeper into the cave.

In the next instant, falling rocks obliterated the fire, and we stumbled back into the darkness, expecting the roof of the cave to fall in on us at any moment.

Just as quickly as it arose, the trembling and shuddering of the mountain subsided. We were all clustered together in the darkness. ''Easy,'' I muttered. ''Easy. It's stopped.''

I struck a match. The dim glow punched a welcome hole in the darkness. Margaret's face was taut with fear, her eyes wide with alarm. I forced an unfelt grin. ''We're going to be okay now.'' I moved the match to illumine Sam's face. ''Just be calm.''

Sam looked around frantically. ''Where's Mutt?'' His eyes grew wide. ''You don't think he's under all of those rocks, do you?''

''No. He was outside with me. He got after a rabbit.'' I nodded to the wall of rocks. ''He's out there, safe.'' I crossed my fingers.

The boy grinned weakly.

Shoelink touched my arm. "*Sangsu*. Stick help. More fire." He held up two dry branches, which ignited easily enough, although they didn't put out much light. Still, we were making progress.

"Here." I gave Sam and Margaret each a burning stick and struck another match. "Let's see what's around here."

We were in luck. There was enough dry branches for us to build a small fire, but once the fire had burned itself out. . . . "All right. Now listen. Shoelink, you and Sam take a burning branch and move back into the cave. Pick up whatever will burn. I'm heading back to the front. I want to see if there's a way out."

"What happened, Gil?" Margaret asked. "Earthquake?"

Despite our ominous situation, I couldn't help noticing this was the first time she had called me Gil. "I don't think so. I'm not saying it wasn't, but I've never heard of earthquakes around here. It could have been, but I'll give you odds it was John Howard's bunch, and when I get out of here, someone is going to pay."

"I'll go with you," she said. "I mean, back to the front of the cave."

I arched an eyebrow, and she added. "I don't want to stay here by myself." She looked around the dark cave. "I'd feel better with you."

"Okay." I nodded to Shoelink. "Don't go too far."

The frail-appearing Oriental peered up at me, shadows from the flickering flames splashing about his thin face. "I understand, *Sangsu*. Not far."

Sam whispered. "I sure wish Mutt was here."

With Margaret trailing behind, I made my way back to the mouth of the cave. In the darkness, we caught a glimpse of coals from the fire. Beyond was a wall of stone, from floor to ceiling.

Extending the small torch, I inspected the cave-in and muttered a curse. "No way we're going out through there."

Margaret caught her breath. "I can't stay in here. I've got to get out."

"Easy, easy. We're going to get out. Just don't worry. We're okay. And we will find a way out. Believe me." She looked up into my eyes, her own glittering with fear. "Trust me. We're going to make it."

She shuddered. "Oh, Gil, I hope so. I hope so."

Chapter Eleven

I studied the remnants of our fire. My hopes surged, for Shoelink had used some dried greasewood to start the fire. Although the wood put off a thick black smoke and a rank stench, it also gave off a bright and long-lasting flame.

Kneeling, I searched along the edges of the still smoldering coals until I found an unburned, foot-long branch. I touched my flickering torch to it, and within seconds, a bright flame leaped from the end of the brand.

Margaret smiled weakly. I nodded to the torch. "Look on the bright side. We got more light."

It was a poor effort to ease her fears, but I couldn't think of anything else to say. "We best get back."

She stopped me. "Gil. What are we going to do? If we can't get out this way, what are we going to do?" Her bottom lip quivered.

I didn't have an answer, at least, not one that would make her feel any better. "We're going to try. That's all I can say. If we can't find a way out, then we'll come back here and dig ourselves out."

"What about the torches . . . what if they go out?"

I smiled grimly at her. "Then we dig in the darkness."

Shoelink and Sam were waiting back at the small fire. Sam's face was pale and tight with fear. The diminutive Oriental's expression was no different from every day for the past seven months we'd been partnering. He motioned to me. "*Sangsu* and Missy come." He pointed down the cave. "Boy and Zhou Gui Ling find way."

Margaret grabbed my arm and stared at Sam. "A way out? Are you sure? Is Shoelink right?"

Sam shrugged. "I don't know. We found a puddle of water in the cave, and there was an opening above it where the rain dripped down, but it was too dark to see up through there."

Shoelink nodded emphatically and waved his skinny arms over his head. "Rain come from sky. We climb up, and we climb out."

I grinned at Margaret. "Well, what are we waiting for? Let's take a look."

A quarter of a mile deep in the cave, we found the pool of water in the middle of the floor. I sloshed into it and peered up into the opening in the ceiling. It was as black as the inside of a cow.

I held the greasewood torch over my head, but the blazing flame only illumined the first few feet of the chimney. I heard a noise, like crumbling dirt. From time to time, the flame flickered, indicating a draft.

"What do you think, Gil?" Margaret's voice was thin with worry.

"Can't tell." I waded back out of the ankle-deep pool. "The sun's up. If we had a straight shot here, we could see the sunlight, but chances are this chimney twists and turns. The only way to see what's up there is to climb it."

"I'll climb it." Sam volunteered. "You might be too big."

I chuckled. "Might be, boy."

"I can do it, Gil. I can climb out and go for help."

"Easy, son. That chimney there could twist around like a snake. You could get yourself hung in there."

Sam gulped, and his pale face turned even whiter.

"No. He isn't going," exclaimed Margaret. "If he got caught up there, we could never get him out."

Before I could reply, a splash in the pool of water behind me solved the argument. I spun and held out the torch. An angry rattlesnake coiled quickly in the water and struck out at us.

Margaret screamed and leaped back.

I shucked my six-gun and calmly blew the snake's head off. The echo within the cave was deafening. My ears rang.

A second rattler fell. I shot it and waited. No more fell.

Taking a deep breath, I shook my head and holstered my side arm. That was the noise I had heard. I deliberately skirted the pool of water. "Well, I reckon that settles that question. Only a cockeyed fool with a death wish would venture up there."

Sam cleared his throat. "What . . . What do we do now, Gil?"

"Well, boy," I replied, pointing the torch toward the back of the cave. "I reckon we'll just have to find out where this here cave takes us."

For what seemed like hours, we trudged deeper and deeper into the cave. I kept an eye on the torch, not only to get a handle on how much time we had left, but to see if there was a draft in the cave.

The floor was thick with dust undisturbed for centuries. As far as I could tell, no one had ever come this far back in the cave. Finally, we stopped to rest. Sam sagged to his knees. Margaret leaned against the wall. Shoelink simply squatted in the middle of the tunnel.

The torch only had a few inches remaining. I was holding it with my thumb and forefinger.

Margaret spotted me eying the burning brand. ''What happens when it goes out?''

I forced a chuckle and held out my hand. ''We feel our way.''

Sam looked over his shoulder. ''What if we have to go back in the dark? What if more snakes fell from the hole?''

For several moments, I looked the boy in the eyes. ''Well, son. . . . that's one of those things I sure hope doesn't come about, but if it does, we'll just have to face it when we get there.'' I patted my shirt pocket. ''But I still have a pocketful of matches, so chances are we'll be out of here before we run out. Okay?'' Another lie. I had five matches.

He swallowed hard and nodded. ''O . . . Okay.''

Thirty minutes later, the torch burned out, plunging us into darkness. Margaret gasped. Quickly, I lit one of my remaining five matches. ''Now, listen. Grab hands. We'll feel our way forward.'' Before anyone could ask the question, I added. ''We've got to save the matches.''

Margaret's hand tightened on mine, and I led us into the darkness, praying for a breeze to chill the sweat on my face, hoping my feet didn't touch the firm yet flexible body of a rattlesnake.

I lost track of time, measuring our existence by the number of matches remaining. A second was struck when the roof of the cave began to drop, forcing us to shuffle forward in a crouch, and then a third when the floor of the cave angled sharply down. The trail was so steep, we had to scoot down on our behinds.

Two matches remained. Only two. Two fragile matches that could prove to be the light of our entire world.

My own hopes were fading, and then we hit a dead end.

I cursed, feeling along the wall, my fingers searching for a corner. There were none.

"What does it mean, Gil?" Sam's voice trembled, struggling to hold back the tears.

I took a deep breath, hoping to hold my own voice steady. "Well, son. It appears we made us a long trip in one direction, and now we're going to have to go back."

No one replied, but I could hear Margaret's quick, shallow breaths, and finally, Sam's response. "Oh."

Suddenly, something hit my leg. I shouted and jumped, and then I heard Mutt barking.

"It's Mutt," Sam shouted in the darkness. "Mutt's in here."

We all babbled in excitement, and I decided it was time to use the next-to-last match.

The welcome glow faintly lit the cave. Mutt was bouncing up and down, licking Sam's face like it was covered with pork grease, and Shoelink hopped around like he was dancing on coals.

At the bottom of the wall was an opening, about three feet high. "Look," I shouted above the laughter. "This must be where he came from." I knelt and held the match near the floor. Sure enough, there were Mutt's tracks leading in.

I grinned at Margaret. "All we have to do is follow him out."

She eyed the small tunnel. "Through that?"

"If he made it, so can we."

"What about snakes?" Sam spoke up.

"Mutt goes first. I follow. Margaret, you come behind me, then Sam, and Shoelink, you bring up the rear."

"Ai. Zhou Gui Ling follow. We go out."

The match burned down to my fingers. I dropped it, and

the darkness returned. "Okay. Everyone on his knees." I took a deep breath.

Everyone has a secret fear, and mine was the horror of being inside a tunnel on my stomach and the roof caving in, pinning me helplessly to the ground, unable to gain any leverage to free myself.

But I had no choice now. I had to go. "Come here, Mutt. Here."

The dog obeyed. I held the scruff of his neck with one hand, and found the tunnel with the other. "Okay, boy. Let's go. Out." I pushed him into the tunnel. Before he could squirm back out, I wedged my bulk in behind him.

Whining, he tried to edge around me, but when he couldn't, Mutt turned back out the tunnel. I followed, my eyes closed, my breathing hard and shallow. Easy, I kept telling myself. Easy, easy, easy. I hoped and prayed the tunnel would not narrow so that we had to back out.

"How is everyone back there?" I asked, my voice sounding strange to my ears.

"Fine. It's sure dark," added Sam.

The boy was dead right about that.

"I'm okay," replied Margaret, her voice breaking. "What about you?"

"No problem," I said, still wondering just what I was going to do if Mutt stumbled on a nest of rattlesnakes. I had one match left. Not much help in a situation like that. "Let's go, Mutt. Get us out of here, boy."

My knees grew sore, and the rocky floor lacerated my hands. Soon, my neck and shoulder cramped from keeping my head cocked up at an angle. I lost track of time.

Just one hand after another, one knee after another, one breath after another—over and over and over. I did my best to suppress the panic welling in me.

"Do you see anything?" Margaret's voice had a hollow ring to it.

"Not yet." Ahead, I could hear Mutt sniffing and scrabbling through the tunnel. How that hound ever managed to find us, I'll never know. I had no way of estimating distance, but I guessed we'd traveled at least a half mile.

My hopes surged when I sensed the trail begin ascending. Around a bend, a chill breeze swept across my face. I almost shouted for joy. We were close to the entrance.

Five minutes later, a small circle of light appeared. "There it is. Just ahead," I yelled back over my left shoulder. "Another couple minutes, and we're out."

I crawled as fast as I could, ignoring my raw knees and hands. All I wanted to do was escape the crushing walls of the narrow passage.

When I rolled outside, I lay on my back and sucked in great breaths of fresh, clean air, savoring the heat of the sun. Moments later, Margaret, Sam, and Shoelink joined me while Mutt bounced over us, barking and licking our faces.

Overhead a hawk screeched, jerking me back to the matters at hand. I rolled to my feet. The sun was directly overhead, which meant we had been in the cave about six or seven hours.

Where were the hombres who had set off the explosion? And the herd and our stock? Were they still there, or had the rustlers pushed them out?

Chapter Twelve

Thick patches of juniper covered the mountain, but I didn't waste time trying to be silent. If the owlhoots were below, they couldn't have kept from hearing Mutt's frenzied barking, so I shucked my six-gun and stumbled full chisel down the mountainside.

The herd was gone, along with our ponies and the burro. "They made sure to take everything," I muttered as we studied the churned-up ground.

I guessed the herd had been pushed out just after the explosion, for water seeping up from the ground had filled the tracks.

"What now?" Margaret looked up at me. Her worried face was smudged with dirt.

"Simple," I replied. "We go get our herd back."

Sam grinned at Shoelink, but Margaret just gaped.

"We've got the advantage," I explained. "They won't be expecting us. As far as they're concerned, we're still in the cave, so they've got nothing to worry about."

"You think they're taking the herd to San Antone?" asked Sam.

"Maybe." I removed my hat and ran my fingers through my long hair, which sorely needed a shearing. First chance I got, I'd have Shoelink pull out a knife and chop it off. "I don't reckon they'd run them off a bluff or nothing. Everyone back in Hankering knew that your Pa was going to get a sizable sum for the critters. So, yeah. My guess is they'll keep on toward San Antone, sell the herd, and split the take.''

Margaret frowned up at me. ''You figure it was someone from Hankering?''

I stared after the herd for several seconds, then nodded to her. ''Yep. I figure it was someone from Hankering.'' I could see in her eyes that she knew who I suspected.

''I still can't believe John Howard is behind this.''

''Maybe not.'' I shrugged. ''But who else has a reason? This way, he gets what he wants and comes out ahead three times. He gets the herd, the money, and the ranch without paying a cent.''

''The ranch?''

''Sure. All he's got to do is come up with a bill of sale. After all, who could disprove a bill of sale if the seller couldn't be found? And,'' I added, ''who can find us buried in a cave?''

For once, Margaret was at a loss for words. All she could do was shake her head. I almost felt sorry for her.

Sam broke the silence. ''What do we do about the rustlers now, Gil? Huh? What do we do? Can I help?''

I grinned at the boy. Actually, he wasn't a boy. He was turning into a young man. ''We'll see. Right now, I don't know what we can do. I won't know until we find the herd.''

Shoelink nodded, and pushed out after the herd, waving for us to follow. I knew we wouldn't have any trouble finding the herd. It couldn't be more than just a few miles ahead. With luck, we could jump the rustlers after they bedded for the night.

The countryside grew rougher, which was in our favor, allowing us to draw closer to the herd unseen. We had more than enough water from the small streams coursing through the rocks, but our stomachs soon started growling. The stew from the night before was down to our toes.

We nibbled on blackberries and wild plums. Shoelink dug up starchy herbs and bulbs from around small ponds. But still our stomachs rumbled.

Just after dark, we spotted a fire in the distance. We had stopped on the side of a hill that afforded us a view of the terrain ahead. "There they are," I whispered, noting the mesa rising beyond them, and wondering why they had not covered more ground. They had moved less than five miles, about half of our daily travel.

"Are you sure?"

I looked at her. "Who else could it be? The herd passed at the bottom of this hill, headed in that direction. But don't worry. I'm not taking any chances. You three stay here. I'll go ahead just to be sure."

Sam frowned. "But Gil, I wanted to go with you."

"You will, boy, you will. But right now, I'm not sure what's out there. I've got to have a chance to find out just what we're facing, then we'll know what to do. Understand?"

Reluctantly, he nodded. "Yeah."

"Okay." I turned to Shoelink. "No fire, unless you put it out of sight on the other side of the crest. Up here on the hill, we're in plain sight. I'll be back later."

There was no moon, but the stars provided enough light so I could pick my way through the juniper and mesquite without raising a ruckus.

Four cowpokes squatted around the fire, but there were nine ponies picketed nearby, counting our three. That meant two other jaspers had to be somewhere around. I was about a hundred feet from the fire, on my belly behind a small juniper, and determined to go no closer. Moments later, a cowpoke appeared from the underbrush and squatted. That left one. Was he with the herd on the other side of the fire?

Of course not, not without a horse. I pressed deeper into the shadows. That meant another was around somewhere. Slowly, I scooted backward, back into the night.

Six was too many. With four, there was a fair possibility of taking them. I could get the drop on them long enough for Shoelink and Sam to take their side arms, but six—too risky.

Backing away, I made a wide circle around the herd to scout the terrain ahead. I wasn't certain what I sought. All I knew was I'd recognize it when I found it.

Thirty minutes later, I paused in a narrow pass. Juniper and mesquite grew thickly along the rimrock, and over a dozen live oaks extended twisted limbs beyond the rim.

An idea flashed into my head. With a crooked grin, I reached for my knife.

I finished my job just after midnight and hurried back to camp, where Shoelink was sitting patiently beside the fire. Gently, I awakened Margaret and Sam out of a sound slumber.

Quickly, I explained the plan.

Margaret frowned, but Sam grinned.

By the time the sun rose, we were ready, high on the rim overlooking the pass below.

"Remember," I cautioned them, "after you push the boulders off, stay up here on the rim, away from the edge. If this doesn't work, they'll potshot anything they see moving." I pointed to a rocky hill two hundred yards to the north. "There's a place up there to hide if you have to." I paused. "You sure you understand?"

Sam nodded eagerly.

Margaret swallowed hard. "Yes."

"I sure would like to see them," Sam said, grinning broadly. "They're sure going to get a surprise."

I gave them a reassuring grin. "I hope so. Let's get on with it. The sun will be up shortly. These fellers might be early risers."

They weren't.

The sun was two hands above the horizon when the herd finally moved out. For two hours I had squatted in a patch of underbrush waiting for them to get started, and for two hours I had grimaced against the cramps threatening to stiffen every muscle in my legs.

Slowly, the herd began to move, browsing slowly forward. I smiled to myself, immediately understanding why the herd had made so little progress the day before. The rustlers were just like me seven months earlier. They knew absolutely nothing about goats. They had a point man, four flankers, and two in drag, exactly the kind of organization for a cattle drive, but all they succeeded in doing was scattering the goats.

The only reason the herd made any progress at all was not because it was being driven, but because it was browsing forward, and if some of the goats decided to browse off in a different direction, they did.

Slowly, the herd fed toward the pass.

I checked my six-gun, hoping my plan worked. If the rustlers decided to turn back on me, I was in big trouble.

The point rider entered the pass, then reined up and turned back to watch in disgust as the critters slowly browsed forward. Gradually, the pass began to fill with goats and riders. When the herd was halfway through, I fired, deliberately aiming at the rocky walls of the pass, intending the slug to ricochet and whine.

The shot echoed across the valley, sending the herd into a run through the pass. I glanced at the rim and spotted Sam peering over the edge. The riders wheeled around, firing blindly in my direction. I fired again.

I wish I could say I tried to wound them, but the truth is, at that a distance, my aim was poor as Job's turkey. I just hoped I could get the slug near them, close enough to spook the owlhoots into making a run for it. I gave a fast prayer.

Someone up there must have heard me, for the bullet clipped off a dead branch that fell on the rump of one of the rustler's horses, spooking the animal and sending it racing through the pass with the herd of goats. The other riders hesitated, confused, then wheeled about and followed their compadre.

In the next instant, several boulders, fastened to the end of slender grapevines, fell over the rim and swung like pendulums down at the riders. One outlaw dodged an oncoming boulder, then reined up his pony and spun to fire back at me, but just as he turned, the boulder swung back, knocking him for a somersault over the head of his pony.

The half dozen boulders swinging from the limbs of the live oaks unnerved the outlaws, sending them hightailing it into the scrub forest of juniper and mesquite.

One headed for me. I managed to hit him in the shoulder, sending him tumbling. He struck the ground and bounced to his feet. Seconds later, he disappeared into the surrounding undergrowth, his lanky legs carrying him as fast as they could.

We ended up with two horses and the burro. Immediately, I checked the brands, and to my surprise, neither was the Slash Bar, John Howard's brand.

I gave Sam the burro to lead and put him with Shoelink at the head of the herd. One pony I gave to Margaret. "Just stay within sight of Shoelink and Sam," I said. "I'll be back later."

She frowned. "Where are you going? We have the goats."

I patted the dun I was riding. "They still have Ned."

An hour later, I caught up with two of the rustlers near a small pool. Ned stood tied to a mesquite. For a moment, I considered getting the drop on the two owlhoots, but decided not to risk gunfire. I backed the dun deeper into the underbrush and whistled.

An answering whinny came from Ned and moments later, the two outlaws started yelling as Ned broke away and headed for me. I whistled again.

Moments later, he pulled up, nuzzling at my extended hand.

Back in the underbrush, I heard the owlhoots stomping and cursing. I threw a couple shots in their direction, sending them stomping and cursing back in the other direction.

I scratched Ned behind the ears. "Miss me, old fella? Reckon you couldn't figure out who was on your back, huh?"

He whinnied, and I climbed from my pony onto Ned's back. "Let's go, old feller." I clicked my tongue, and we started back to the herd.

The two horses we took from the rustlers provided us with two more Winchesters, three in all. In one saddlebag, we discovered two boxes of .44 cartridges, so we were in fair shape as far as firepower was concerned.

"You think we'll need all this?" Margaret gestured to the hardware that night when we camped.

"Hard to say, but I reckon when Howard's boys tell him what happened, he'll come gunning for us with blood in his eyes.'' I sipped my coffee and wolfed down some beans.

''I still don't think he had anything to do with the rustling. We've known him for years.''

I shrugged, not anxious to argue. ''I could be wrong. The horses we got from these rustlers didn't have his brand, and that owlhoot back in the draw might have stolen that horse from Howard. But whoever is behind this won't stop.'' I gulped down the last of my coffee and picked up my Winchester.

She arched an eyebrow. ''For all you know, these rustlers might not even be the same ones who stampeded the herd before. You might have scared the first ones off, and if you did, they won't come back.''

All I could do was look at her and shake my head.

At that moment, Shoelink appeared from the darkness. I winked at him. ''I'll take over now.''

''What about me, Gil?'' Sam spoke up. ''When is it my turn to take over the watch?''

I grinned at the boy, then brushed him off. ''Later, son. Later.''

He stuck out his jaw. ''But, I'm almost thirteen. I can help. I want to help. These are my goats.''

Neither Shoelink nor Margaret said a word, but they were both watching the two of us with amused curiosity. The laughter in her eyes got under my skin. I wasn't right sure how to handle a boy like this. On the one hand, he was like a young colt, tugging at the bit. Too rough, I could break his spirit. Too easy, he could hurt himself.

I cursed Wash Cottle for breaking his neck. This was his responsibility, not mine.

''Isn't that right?'' Sam insisted. ''These are my goats. I oughta be able to help.''

For a moment, I studied him. One thing was certain, he

and I needed some kind of understanding between us. I swung onto Ned's back and stared down at Sam. "We'll talk in the morning. I reckon there's some merit in what you say. I don't have time tonight, but tomorrow, we'll iron things out."

Without giving the boy a chance to argue, I dug my heels into Ned's flanks and rode out into the darkness, glad to get away from the camp, out into the cool night where all I had to worry about were rustlers, rattlesnakes, and rank-smelling goats.

Mutt followed me into the night and tagged along behind as I slowly circled the herd, which I had learned the first few nights was an unnecessary task, but one I continued just because I felt as if I had to do something.

I had never pushed animals anywhere without watching over them at night, from water hole to water hole, from pasture to pasture, from ranch to ranch. I didn't trust the goats. At least, that was the story I made myself believe so I wouldn't feel too much the fool traipsing around a herd of critters who, I knew deep down, had no intention of going anywhere until daylight.

All night I rode, snatching bits of sleep in the saddle when I wasn't trying to figure out just what to do with the boy. One fact was certain. He was almost thirteen. In the West, that was right on the edge of manhood.

I reined up and looked over the sleeping herd. What in the blazes was I doing out here at three o'clock in the morning watching over a bunch of critters that weren't going anywhere? Why couldn't the boy do it? Let him lose sleep. I chuckled to Mutt who was looking up at me and whining. "I reckon he wouldn't be so all-fired anxious after a night out here without sleep. Don't you figure?"

Mutt cocked his head and barked softly.

With a click of my tongue, I sent Ned on around the herd. "That's just what I'll do." I grinned. "Tomorrow night, Sam gets to be a man."

"He can't." Margaret glared at me. "He's too young to be out there all night by himself."

Her barrage caught me by surprise. I figured she'd like the idea. "Well, it isn't like he's all by himself out there. Mutt's with him. And we're right here. No more than a whoop and a holler."

Sam joined in. "Nothing's going to happen to me, Miss Margaret. Honest. Besides, I'll only be out there a few hours. What could happen?"

For a fleeting moment, despair wrinkled her forehead, but determination quickly replaced it. "Anything. Indians, outlaws, maybe even a panther after a goat."

I smirked. "The Indians are on the reservation."

"That's how much you know," she shot back. "They don't stay there all the time. They're always coming and going. And what about the rustlers? You said they would come back. What if they come back when Sam's out there? Huh? You stop to think about that, Smarty-Pants?"

I stared at her, unable to believe my ears. She was ignoring her argument about the rustlers and throwing my accusations back in my face. Besides, the night before, when Sam was pushing to help, she said nothing—in effect, supporting him. And now, when I finally give in, she yells loud enough to wake snakes.

A sense of frustration washed over me. Was there any way to keep everyone happy? I didn't reckon so.

"What about it, Gil?" Sam tugged on my sleeve. "Huh? Can I still go?"

I sighed, wondering how I managed to end up in the middle of all this. I was just a drifter, a down-at-the-heels drifter passing through. No responsibilities, no obligations, no commitments. And now, without warning, I had a unpredictable herd, a jabbering boy, a puzzling Oriental, and a baffling woman on my hands. Oh, and I forgot. A three-legged dog also.

"What about it, Gil? Huh, huh?"

In a flash, I made up my mind.

First, I wasn't planning on sticking around West Texas.

Second, I was headed for the Tetons.

Third, why should I care what anyone thought, especially her?

Fourth, I was tired of watching a herd that didn't need looking after.

Fifth, I was doing a man's job when I was twelve.

Sixth, why couldn't Sam do the same thing? And—

Seventh, no woman was going to tell me what to do.

I looked at Sam. "You ride herd tonight, boy."

"Yippeee," he shouted, waving his hat over his head.

Chapter Thirteen

I wish I could say Miss Margaret accepted my decision and behaved grown-up about it, but I can't. After Sam rode out that night, six inches of ice settled over the camp. The norther that me and Shoelink weathered back in the early winter was a spring nipper compared to the frosty chill she laid on us.

She didn't say a word that evening. The clanging and battering of the pots and pans spoke more eloquently of her displeasure than words.

Even Shoelink, usually so complacent and withdrawn that he seemed to be outside looking in, disappeared into the darkness, undoubtedly spreading his soogan under a nearby juniper, as far away from her none-too-subtle wrath as possible.

I slept but little, waking every few minutes, cursing myself for my own stubbornness. I had been determined not to let anyone make up my mind for me, and now I was paying the piper. "Serves you right, knothead," I muttered, slipping from my blankets and stoking up the fire. "Serves you blasted well right."

After a cup of steaming coffee, I rode out to relieve Sam.

"No problems, Gil. None at all," he exclaimed.

That was a weight off my shoulders. "Get on back and fill your stomach, boy. We're moving out before the sun."

The grin on his face erased the consternation Margaret's

icy silence had raised. I should have known. I was right. There was nothing out here to hurt the boy, nothing at all.

The next few days were the most uncomfortable I had ever spent. Margaret spoke in monosyllables, so cold a man had to chip away the ice to understand her. I came to seriously doubt that she and I would ever again exchange more than three or four words at any one sitting.

Sam continued nighthawking with me. At first, I considered keeping him in camp, but I recognized the gesture as simply a hypocritical effort to salve Margaret's anger. The damage was done. Nothing I did would change it, so I might as well keep blundering straight ahead, giving Sam more responsibility.

We kept pushing the herd, Shoelink padding along at point with the bell goat, the rest of us bringing up the rear or watching the flanks.

Each day, I expected the rustlers to return, and each day passed without incident. Maybe Margaret had been right. Maybe the rustlers had given up.

The unfriendly terrain grew rougher, slashed by rocky gullies and dotted by hilltops choked with juniper and scrub oak so thick that in places the goats passed single file.

After two more days of such grueling travel, we were near exhaustion. That was when the wolf packs hit.

The first strike came a couple of hours before sunup one morning.

Rifle fire from the direction of the herd jerked me from my blankets. The howl of the wolves sent chills down my spine. I grabbed my Winchester and ran toward the herd. Sam was firing steadily from the back of his pony.

I skidded to a halt on a ledge overlooking the valley in which we had bedded the goats. The frightened animals milled about, a brown and white carpet jittering nervously in the moonlight. A sudden hole appeared in the carpet as the goats scattered from the wolves, then filled back in as the predators passed.

Without hesitation, I began firing, aiming for the fleeting shadows zigzagging through the herd. On the far side of the goats, Sam continuing firing. Goats bleated. Wolves snarled.

Margaret joined me, firing steadily.

As quickly as they appeared, the wolves vanished, unnerved by the three Winchesters pumping lead into them. The goats continued milling about. I shouted across the valley to Sam. "Start circling again, boy. Reload, and keep circling. Steady the critters down."

In the darkness beyond the herd, we heard the growls and snarls as the pack tore apart the hapless goats it had dragged away. I glanced at Margaret.

The faint moonlight revealed the alarm on her face. "Will they be back?"

"They'll be back," I said, turning my attention back to the wolves. "Maybe not tonight, but they'll be back. You can take that to the bank. They'll be back."

We pushed out before sunrise, but not before there was enough light to count seven dead wolves, long, gaunt creatures with sunken bellies and razor-sharp teeth. I shook my head at the number of dead. "Large pack."

No one replied, but Shoelink moved a little faster that day.

I remained at drag, Winchester in hand, my eyes constantly searching the brush around us for any sign of the wolves.

"How many goats did we lose, Gil?" Sam pulled in beside me.

"Hard to say, boy. From the sounds of feeding last night, there was a sizable number of wolves left."

Margaret pulled her pinto up beside us and glanced over her shoulder. Her earlier anger with me was forgotten. "Will they come after us?"

"You mean, us . . . you and me?"

"Yes."

"No. Don't worry about that." I gestured to the herd. "Not with the number of critters we got here. They'll tag along and snatch one when they can."

At the time, I had no idea how wrong I was.

I just continued babbling. "But unless we kill them off or get rid of them someway, we'll have them all the way to San Antone."

Shoelink kept the herd moving, skipping our routine noon stop. I grinned. I didn't blame him. I rode up beside the small Oriental and dismounted, falling into step with him.

"We need valley, high valley," I said, first spreading my arms as if I were trying to pick up a barrel, then holding one hand high over my head. "High walls in a circle."

He frowned. "Wolves go in. Goats no run. No run."

"Yeah." I nodded. "And the wolves can't run." I pointed my finger like a six-gun. "Wolves no run. We shoot wolves."

His frown turned into a grin. He nodded emphatically. "Ah. Yes. Wolves no run. We shoot. Boom, boom."

"Yes. Boom, boom."

That was our plan, but we could not find a suitable spot to ambush the wolves before dark. "Maybe tomorrow," I said as we threw our gear under an overhanging ledge and put together kindling for a fire.

"You'll need help out there tonight, Gil." Sam patted his Winchester.

"Not tonight, Sam. The land is too flat. Last night, we could stand above the herd, but tonight . . . well, I want you three to stay here under the ledge . . . out of the way of any wild slugs.''

Sam shook his head. "What if the wolves come after you?''

"They won't. Not with the goats around. They'll slip into the herd and pull out what they can. Ned and me will hang around the edge, keep the goats in place. I'll probably get us a few wolves like that. Maybe tomorrow we'll find the spot we're looking for.''

Margaret stopped me. "Be careful,'' she said.

I winked at her. "Believe me. Those varmints are a lot more scared of me than I am of them. All you got to do is holler, and they'll go running.'' I nodded to the fire. "Just keep the fire going. I don't expect the wolves to come around here, but in case some stray in this direction, the fire will keep them away.''

Shoelink nodded. "We keep big fire, *Sangsu*. Big fire.''
"You do that.''

If we'd known then what was going to happen later that night, I would have insisted they build a bonfire.

The first couple of hours after dark were uneventful. An occasional wolf howled, that mournful ululating wail that raised the hackles on the back of the neck, but a .44 slug in its direction always silenced it. Ned and me slowly circled the herd. Ned was on edge tonight, his ears perked forward. He knew what was out there.

Around ten o'clock, the moon rose, bathing the herd and underbrush in a pale white glow. The goats were nervous, gathering in clusters, facing out. Because the terrain was so flat, I couldn't see more than forty or fifty yards into the surrounding junipers and mesquite.

Then I spotted the first shadow, a fleeting streak of black that disappeared behind the blurred silhouette of a juniper. Another shadow followed, then another. Off to the left, a flicker of motion caught my eye.

More shadows.

And then the guttural growls of the wolves broke the silence.

I jerked the Winchester to my shoulder and fired above the silent phantoms. Some veered, then cut back toward the herd. I fired again, but the shots didn't seem to affect the animals.

"Yip, yip, yip." I shouted and spurred Ned through the herd toward the shadows, standing in the stirrups and firing into the approaching pack. I glanced to the right, and my muscles stiffened.

Dark apparitions too numerous to count raced through the underbrush toward the herd. My heart thudded against my chest. I couldn't even begin to count the number. They were like a black flood covering the ground. There might have been fifty, maybe a hundred, certainly more than I had ever seen at one time.

Like a giant wave, they hit the herd, scattering it, tearing into the frightened goats. Jerking Ned around, I raced toward the nearest pack of wolves, firing rapidly. In the next second, I was among them, but they didn't break and run.

Instead, they dodged and snarled, leaping for me, reaching for Ned. Abruptly, the hammer clicked on an empty chamber, so I used the muzzle of the Winchester like a club, trying to drive the wolves away. They leaped and snapped, driven to a frenzy by the smell of fresh blood.

One sunk his teeth into Ned's neck and clung tenaciously when the frightened horse reared and lashed out with his front hooves. I clubbed the wolf, knocking him senseless.

Immediately, I wheeled Ned around and sent him racing

through the herd, out of harm's way. On the far side of the herd, I pulled up to a live oak, the bottom branch almost ten feet above the ground. I pulled myself onto the broad limb and slapped Ned on the rump, sending him back to the camp, hoping his unexpected appearance would put the others on guard.

From my perch, I fired at the wolves, which were slowly breaking apart the herd, sending the goats scattering across the countryside in fear.

"You blasted varmints," I muttered between clenched teeth. "I'll see every last one of you in Hades." I fired again.

The rifle barrel grew hot, then sizzling.

Slowly, the wolves drove the herd under my limb and then on into the shrub forest. In the bleak light of the fading moon, dark shadows dotted the ground. Guttural snarls echoed from the darkness as savage wolves glutted their bellies.

Suddenly, a deep-throated growl sounded directly behind me. I froze, my mind racing. Before I could turn, I heard the scrape of claws on bark. Instantly, I fell forward on the limb.

Sharp claws hit my back, scraped across my head, and then startled yaps sounded from the branch before me. I jerked up and saw a snarling wolf hanging from the fork of the limb with his front legs, clawing madly with his hind paws to pull himself back up on the limb.

I clubbed him across the head with the Winchester.

He hit the ground and yelping, disappeared into the night.

My heart was beginning to slow back down. I swallowed hard and looked over my shoulder, noting the limb on which I sat arched to the ground, providing an unhindered path up to me.

Suddenly, gunfire erupted in the direction of camp. I cursed, grateful I'd insisted they build a fire in front of the ledge.

By now, the herd had scattered into the night. From every direction came growls and snarls, pitiful bleating and frightened squeals. I looked around. I was stuck in this tree until dawn.

But not on this limb. Steadying myself, I rose to my feet and then clambered another ten feet up the tree, settling myself in a fork so that if I should doze, I wouldn't fall. To make doubly certain, I looped my belt around the trunk, then through the arms of my vest, which I then buttoned snugly about my chest.

Throughout the remainder of the night, occasional wolves sniffed under the tree, picked up my scent, and growled into the dark patches of leaves overhead.

Only one started up the limb, and when I fired in his direction, he went scrambling and yelping into the night.

As false dawn lightened the sky, I began to get a better idea of the damage the wolves had inflicted the night before. Not as much as I expected. There were a few goats sprawled about, but most had been carried away by the wolves.

I eased to the ground and, Winchester loaded and cocked, headed back to the camp. My eyes moved continuously, searching the undergrowth, studying the terrain, watching my back trail. I stayed close to trees, just in case I had to swing into one. My heart thudded against my chest, and my throat was drier than a year-old bale of hay.

But I reached the camp without incident.

Sam ran out to meet me. "You okay, Gil? Huh? You okay?" Shoelink and Margaret followed the boy out.

"Yeah." I looked around and lowered the Winchester to

the ground. "I'm fine. How about you three? I heard gunfire."

Margaret forced a smile. "We're safe." She gestured to
the coals in the cave. "Lucky we gathered extra wood.
They smelled the horses. After awhile, they gave up."

My shoulders ached, and my eyes burned. I reached for
the coffee. "Well, reckon we need to see about gathering
the herd." I looked at Shoelink. "I'll go out first . . . see if
any wolves are still around."

He nodded.

Sam patted his Winchester. "You want me to go with
you, Gil?"

I grinned. "No, boy. You stay here and watch after the
camp. You'll get your fill of riding when I get back."

The wolves had vanished, carrying with them their car-
rion. We ran across only about a dozen dead goats while
gathering the herd. "Better than I thought."

Margaret looked at me from the back of her pinto. "How
many did we lose? I mean, besides the ones we found. How
many do you figure the wolves carried off?"

"Hard to say." I eyed the herd.

Shoelink spoke up. "Not many." He held up the fingers
of both hands and flashed them three times. "Not many.
We okay."

Sam and Margaret grinned until I replied. "For the time
being. What about tonight?"

Margaret's forehead wrinkled in a frown. "You mean,
they'll come back? After all this?"

I motioned for Shoelink to lead off. "Wouldn't you?"

She swallowed hard. Her face paled. "They're going to
follow us all the way to San Antonio, like you said?"

"Unless we can figure out how to stop them. Shoelink's
right. We probably lost thirty or forty last night. Now, you

figure. The wolves gorged. The truth is, they probably won't be back tonight. Their bellies are full. They won't be desperate enough to face gunfire. Not tonight.''

"So, when?" Margaret's cheeks were regaining their color.

"Hard to say." I shrugged. "A week, maybe less. I figure they'll hit us at least two, maybe three more times before we reach San Antone. Unless we can find a spot to kill them all.''

And I knew the chances of that were slim.

Chapter Fourteen

We hit the Pecos River the next day, midafternoon. After watching the herd's reaction every time a storm blew over the horizon, I had a sneaky feeling getting those critters across the river was not going to be just a stroll in the meadow.

I was right. The herd balked; like a hardheaded mule, it sat on its collective haunches and refused to move. I rode up beside Shoelink and took the lead rope, pulling the bell goat after me into the river.

The frightened doe rolled her eyes and bleated pitifully, struggling against the rope. I figured if I got her in the water, the others would follow.

So much for my goat wisdom.

On the far shore, I looked back. The goats remained fixed on the shore, stubbornly refusing to enter the water. I glanced down at the wet goat, then swam back, dragging her with me.

Margaret arched an eyebrow as I dismounted. "Now what?"

I shook my head, wishing Wash Cottle was here. He would have known what to do. I sure didn't, so I made a profound observation. "They don't like water."

She rolled her eyes. "I would never have guessed." She chuckled. "You still didn't answer my question. What do we do now?'' Her brown eyes laughed merrily at my quandary.

Behind her, Sam grinned.

I pushed my hat to the back of my head and dragged my shirtsleeve across my forehead. ''Only thing I know to do is head up or down the river, and hope we find a shallow crossing where these blasted critters won't have to swim.''

Margaret nodded. ''Okay. Which way do we go?''

''Well . . .'' I looked north, then back south.

Sam broke in. ''I can ride north, Gil. We still got three or four hours before sundown. Let me ride north, and you can go south. We can meet back here before dark.''

I started to object, but then, I couldn't really figure what I would be objecting to. The boy had a good idea. Save us time all the way around. I glanced at Margaret from the corner of my eye. A frown deeper than the Pecos River was carved in her forehead.

Sam saw the apprehensive glance I gave Margaret. Hastily, he said. ''I'll be careful. Honest, Gil. I promise.''

''I don't know, boy.'' I glanced at the sun. He was right. We had about three hours of daylight, and it did make a heap more sense finding a crossing before pushing the whole herd one way or another just to have to turn around and head back. ''A bunch could happen out there. Most of it bad.''

He patted the butt of his booted Winchester. ''I won't take any chances, Gil. If I see even one wolf, I'll head straight back.''

His suggestion would save time. No question about that. ''Okay, Sam. You ride north about an hour or so. I want you back here before dark, you hear?''

A grin wider than the river leaped to his face. ''I hear, Gil. Don't worry. I'll be back.''

Before I could add another word of caution, he wheeled

his pony around and put it into a trot upriver. I nodded to Shoelink. "Make camp here." I pointed to the bend in the river. "Gather the goats over there. That way, we have the river on three sides."

"Ai, *Sangsu*. Missy and Zhou Gui Ling make fire. Like you say. Not to worry."

"Okay." I glanced at Margaret. "If I don't find a crossing before sundown, I'm going to push on after dark."

Margaret opened her mouth to protest, but I quickly explained. "We've got to find a crossing. There's a moon tonight, not much, but enough. I'll keep on till midnight. That'll cover about twenty miles or so. If I don't find anything by then, I'll head back. We'll push out at first light."

"But, you won't get any sleep."

I winked at her. "Once we get the herd moving, I'll grab a nap in the saddle."

I kept my eyes fixed on the river as I rode downstream, searching for a shallow crossing for the herd. But the river flowed deep and wide for miles. Around five-thirty or so, I reined up and peered on downriver, searching for a large bend or some sweeping curves, anything to indicate the possibility of a shallow crossing.

Nothing.

Stubbornly, I continued, keeping Ned in a walking two-step, a gait that covered ground without jarring a jasper's insides to jelly.

Night settled over the hill country, a blue-black darkness that carried with it the delicate aroma of wild honeysuckle and fragrant jasmine. A warm southern breeze stirred the air, giving it just enough of a chill for comfort.

I looked up at the stars, the Milky Way a white path slashing a broad swath across the heavens. I settled back in my saddle and felt a sense of peace. That sight had been the ceiling of my bedroom for as long as I could remember. More than three-quarters of my twenty-seven years had been spent under the glittering canopy, counting stars instead of sheep.

The Pecos continued its slow journey to the border and its confluence with the Rio Grande. I kept track of time by the Big Dipper, and when it struck midnight, I headed back, disappointed. I had found no crossing for the goats.

"Maybe the boy had some luck," I muttered to Ned as I nudged the roan into a lope back to camp.

Dawn was breaking when I smelled the tang of wood smoke and fresh coffee wafting through the scrub forest. My eyes burned from lack of sleep, but I licked my lips in anticipation of a steaming mug of six-shooter coffee and a plate of hot beans.

Sam jumped up from the campfire when he spotted me. He waved wildly and spoke to Margaret, who was shading her eyes against the rising sun.

He raced up to me even before I pulled Ned to a halt. "I found a crossing, Gil. Upriver, about three miles."

I stared at him in disbelief.

Shoelink nodded, and Margaret grinned.

"It's real shallow, no more than ankle-deep. All gravel."

Margaret spoke up. "You should have seen him. He came riding back in about half an hour after you left. Excited as all get out. Well, Shoelink and me went back with him, and he's right. There is a crossing, between two bluffs. Looks like they caved in and made a dam of sorts. The river's backed up considerable and the water's running over the top. Like Sam said, it's mostly gravel. We walked out on it, and it seemed mighty solid."

I squatted by the fire as they described the dam. I scooped up a few spoonfuls of beans and washed them down with coffee. "Well," I said, rising and dragging the back of my hand across my lips. "Let's get the herd up there."

Sam froze momentarily. "Don't you want to see it first?"

"Why? You saw it, all of you. Can we get the goats across?"

Neither Margaret nor Sam replied. Shoelink spoke. "Take time, but goats cross river."

"Then let's get moving." I swung into the saddle. "We're burning daylight."

I rode ahead to the dam. As they said, the gravel appeared solid, the result of a section of the hundred-foot-high west rim caving in, leaving a dam thirty feet high and twenty feet wide. I rode across. Ned's hooves dug into the gravel, breaking it loose, which allowed the water to carry it away.

"Blast," I muttered, realizing the reason the dam had held was that nothing had broken the caked soil that cemented the gravel together, but now, the sharp hooves of the goats would cut through the gluelike soil and cause the gravel to shift.

Given enough goats, the dam would collapse. Still, we didn't have a choice. We had to get the goats across, and this was our best hope, probably our only hope.

The far side of the dam rose slightly, opening onto the prairie beyond. I dismounted and walked back on the dam, critically inspecting it. On the east side, the clear, cold water ran over the crown at a depth of three or four inches, shallow enough not to spook the goats. On the west, it sluiced down narrow channels to the stream thirty feet below.

I peered upstream at the small lake, wondering just how

much longer the dam could withstand the enormous pressure of all the water backing up. To make our situation even more dangerous, the hooves of each goat would reduce the capability of the dam.

I untied Ned and patted his neck. "Going to be tricky, old son. Mighty tricky."

Ned whinnied and stomped his feet. I tugged gently on the reins. "Easy, boy. Don't go knocking any holes in this dam. There's enough of them critters coming up behind us to do the job." I led him back across the dam, then mounted.

An hour later, Shoelink led the bell goat across. The remainder of the critters followed without hesitation, moving several abreast despite our efforts to narrow the herd. Clannish by nature, the goats scurried to bunch together, forcing those on the perimeter to scramble along the side of the damn. There, the hooves sunk deeply into the gravel, sending it scattering down the steep slope.

Slowly, the herd crossed. Their hooves dug into the gravel, breaking apart each layer of pebbles, sending the small rocks tumbling down the dam and washing downstream. The three-inch overflow grew to four, then five inches.

Shoelink continued east, stringing out the critters behind him in a straggling, twisting line. Goats still waiting to cross bleated mournfully and bunched up at the river's edge, forcing more of the creatures onto the dam and sending more scrabbling along the edges and down the sides.

The critters' hooves dug deeper and deeper into the gravel. The water over the crown increased to six inches.

Margaret sat on her pinto beside me on the west side. "Won't be long now before they're over."

"No. Not long." I noted the depth of water over the

crown of the dam had increased again. "You and Sam better get on over." I nodded to the goats. "Just move in there, in the middle, and get on across."

She looked back at me. Before she could speak, I said, "I'll be right along. I just need you two to keep the goats moving on the other side."

Without argument, she and Sam moved out, slowly crossing the dam. Behind them, goats milled, the worst thing they could do, for their sharp hooves sent more gravel sluicing down into the river below.

There were still a couple hundred goats on my side, so I eased Ned back behind them and pushed as much as I dared, hoping to urge them to move a little faster.

I kept a keen eye on the dam. If it broke, I could swim across, but I wanted to get all the goats over if I could. Any that remained behind would be easy prey for the marauding wolves.

On the far side, Sam wheeled his pony about and whistled at the goats, slapping his hat against his leg in an effort to hurry the critters along.

I had to admit, the boy was a hard worker. A far cry from the frightened little child I had met seven months earlier. And he had learned his business fairly well. He sat his pony easily, he didn't complain about grub or work, and he did what he was told.

Of course, I told myself, turning my attention to Margaret Curtice, I could say the same thing for her, at least since her futile attempt to escape.

For a moment, I allowed myself a few seconds to reflect. "Yeah, we're not such a bad crew after all," I muttered to Ned. "Not bad at all."

By now, the last of the goats had started across. The water was almost eight inches deep across the top of the dam, the current strong enough that the goats almost refused to move, but with me behind, yip, yip, yipping and Mutt yap, yap, yapping, we drove the critters on across.

Just as I urged Ned onto the west shore, Sam shouted. "Look. Another goat, a kid."

Bleating pitifully, a small kid stood on the opposite bank, eyeing first us and then the rushing water. Suddenly, a wrist-thick geyser of water squirted out near the base of the dam.

"I'll get him," shouted the boy, dismounting and dashing across the dam before I could stop him.

Margaret screamed.

"Sam. Get the blazes back here," I shouted above the increasing rush of water. "The dam's fixing to break."

Ignoring me, Sam sloshed through the knee-deep water to the goat and scooped the small critter up in his arms. I muttered a curse and leaped from the saddle. Ned was too heavy for the rapidly deteriorating dam.

Below, another geyser shot out, arching forty feet through the air. I hurried across the dam, stumbling as the gravel swept from under my feet. Sam staggered toward me, his pale face frightened, but he clutched the kid to him like life itself.

I was both angry with and proud of the boy, but I didn't have time to do anything except grab him and shove him ahead of me. Abruptly, my feet fell out from under me as the middle of the dam disappeared into a sinkhole. I glimpsed the sky above, and the next thing I knew, tons of water engulfed me.

Like a giant hand, the water picked me up and hurled me downstream, spinning me head over heels. I held my breath and flailed at the flood.

Suddenly, I popped to the surface and grabbed a fresh breath before I was pulled under again. Every time my feet struck bottom, I kicked toward the shore, but after a few seconds, I was so disoriented, I had no idea in which direction the shore lay. So I just kept kicking.

In the next breath, my head was out of the water. I glimpsed a loop flying through the air in my direction. I stabbed my hand into the air and missed, but the loop whipped around my wrist and almost yanked my arm out of its socket. The next thing I knew, I was being dragged to the shore.

The scrape and scratch of rocks against my skin never felt so good. I lay half in, half out of the river, gasping for breath.

Margaret knelt beside me and laid her hand on my shoulder. "Gil. Gil. Are you all right?"

I managed to nod. "Yeah. Yeah, I think so." I rolled over as she rose and coiled her rope.

She grinned when she saw the puzzled expression on my face as I stared at the rope. "Yes. I'm the one who snagged you. Who'd you think did it, your Chinese friend?"

I closed my eyes and chuckled. I didn't even bother to respond to her question. "Thanks."

"Don't mention it."

Chapter Fifteen

That night, I left Shoelink to look after the camp and stuck Margaret and Sam in trees on either side of the herd in anticipation of the wolves returning.

"I thought you said it'd be about a week before they came back?" She made the remark as she seated herself in the fork of the oak.

"That's what I expect," I replied, poking cartridges in my Winchester. "But we can't take any chances."

The wolves didn't strike that night, nor the next, nor the next.

The fourth night, we camped where Buckhorn Draw and Johnson Creek opened into Dry Devil's Creek. For the first time since the Pecos, I didn't put out guards other than the nighthawk—and I was usually the nighthawk.

"Another three or four days," I said around the campfire that night, "and we'll reach the west fork of the Nueces."

Sam glanced over his shoulder in the direction of the Pecos. "Is it a big river?"

Shoelink caught my eyes, and I spotted a smile in his. "Not like the last, Sam. There hasn't been a whole lot of storms, so I'm hoping it'll be shallow enough for this herd of onery critters to cross without bowing their necks."

Both Sam and Margaret grinned. I didn't have the heart to tell them about the cottonmouth water moccasins.

Beyond the west fork four days ahead, the terrain grew

119

rougher. Half a dozen mountains blocked our way. Though they were small compared to the Rocky Mountains farther west, they still threw up a formidable barrier for the herd, so I planned to swing north around them, hit the upper branches of the Nueces, then follow the river south for about fifty miles. To the best of my calculations, that would put us five days west of San Antone.

"Another twelve to fifteen days," I added, pouring myself another cup of coffee before heading out to nighthawk.

"You mean, before San Antonio?" Sam's eyes danced with excitement.

"Yeah." I winked at Margaret.

"What's it like? I mean, San Antonio. Like Fort Worth?"

I leaned back against the rough bark of a scrub oak. "Well, I reckon they're about the same size. I'm not much of a judge like that, but you got to understand, boy. There's two different cultures there. They act a lot different."

He frowned. "I don't understand. Why's that? They're all Texans, aren't they?"

Margaret laughed. I nodded to her. "You explain it to the boy."

Her eyes twinkled. "You see, Sam, years ago, this was all part of Mexico. The Mexican government sent its armies and priests up here to colonize . . . to settle. For years, Texas was part of Mexico, with all the habits and religion," she said. "Then, about forty years ago, Sam Houston defeated General Santa Ana and Texas became a republic."

Sam's eyebrows knit. "A republic? Is that like a state? My pa said Texas was a state."

"Well, it is . . . at least, now it is. Back then, Texas was an independent country. That's a republic. Davy Crockett and Jim Bowie and Bill Travis, they all liked the idea of men being free to do whatever they chose. That's why they fought Santa Ana, to make Texas a republic.''

Sam scratched his head. ''Then why did Texas become a state? I mean, if everybody could do what they wanted, what good was it to be a state?''

I spoke up. ''You see, Sam, you get a bunch of states together, they all can help each other do a whole lot more than they could do by themselves. They work together to do better for themselves. That's what a democracy is, giving the power to someone to tell us all what to do.''

My explanation puzzled the boy.

''Seems like to me,'' he began. ''That if a state has to listen to other states or other people tell it what it can or can't do, then that's not as good as a republic, where you can do whatever you want.''

We grew silent around the campfire. I looked at Margaret, and she looked at me, neither of us quite sure how to answer Sam's last remark. I knew the answer, but I wasn't sure if I could explain it.

''Sam, back East, I suppose you went into some large businesses at times, places that had a lot of goods to sell and probably cheaper than some of the small stores thereabouts, huh?''

He considered the question a moment, then nodded. ''Yeah. Yeah, there was this big general store, Wiley's Mercantile, and Ma always bought her sewing goods there because she said he was cheaper than the others.''

''Well, that's kind of like states. Mr. Wiley probably purchased his goods with some other merchants. That way, several of them buying together could get better prices than just one small man. States are like that. We're willing to give up the right to do everything we want so we can afford to get things that we all need.''

I cringed when I finished my explanation, for I didn't even understand my answer.

"I don't understand," Sam replied simply.

Shoelink spoke up. "Young master, when the state fight Mexico people, no one from United States come help." He made a sweeping gesture to the east. "Now, we state. Now we fight, everyone come help."

The youngster looked at Shoelink. "You mean, a republic has to do it all on its own, without help from nobody?"

Shoelink nodded emphatically. "Ai. That what Zhou Gui Ling mean. No help from nobody."

For several seconds, Sam stared at the fire. I could see the wheels turning in his head. Finally, he looked at Margaret. "So Texas was a republic and then became a state?"

"Yes." Her eyes gazed into the past. "Sam Houston. He was the one who pushed Texas into the union."

"Don't forget Steve Austin," I said.

Sam frowned at her. "Steve Austin. Who was he?"

Margaret rolled her eyes and held up a hand. "Not tonight. History lesson's over. I'll tell you more tomorrow night."

"Okay." Sam turned to me. "Steve Austin was a good Texan, huh?"

For a moment, I remembered all the stories I'd heard about Steve Austin and all the others. My chest swelled with pride. Would there ever be another band of stalwart patriots like that? "Yeah, son. Steve Austin was a good Texan."

I sipped my coffee. "Ugh." I wrinkled my nose. The coffee was cold. I dumped it on the fire and reached for the pot for one more hot sip before I went out to the herd. A jasper always needed that last shot of hot coffee before nighthawking.

* * *

Each night, we expected the wolves, but they failed to appear. "What do you think happened?" Margaret stared over our back trail the next morning.

I steadied Ned. "Beats me. Maybe we lost them at the river."

"You mean, they lost the trail where the dam broke?" Sam wrinkled his forehead.

Margaret sniffed. "That doesn't seem likely."

"No." I chuckled. "It sure don't, but then, I've come across some mighty unlikely things out here. Let's us just count our blessings, and keep pushing on."

And that's what we did, straight on toward the West Fork of the Nueces and the cottonmouth water moccasins.

The night before we were scheduled to hit the West Fork, I took Shoelink aside and told him what to expect. "All we can do is figure it out when we get there," I said. "I'll ride ahead and try to find a shallow ford where we can get across without disturbing the snakes."

He stared at me several seconds. "Snnnaake?" He made a sinuous movement with his hand and forearm.

"Yes." I curved my index and middle finger. "Bad poison. Kill you, me." I jabbed my curved fingers at him, then at my leg where the diamondback had hit me.

The diminutive Oriental shivered. He stared into the darkness. "Texas really hard country."

I had to agree with Shoelink. Texas was really a hard country.

He nodded to Margaret and Sam, who had spread their blankets by the fire. "*Sangsu* tell Missy and boy about snakes?"

"Nope." I shook my head. "I'll tell them in the morning. No sense in disturbing their sleep tonight."

I rode out early next morning after breaking the news to

Margaret and Sam. "If I can find the right ford, maybe we can move the entire herd across without disturbing the snakes."

Margaret took another sip of her coffee, then spit it out. She'd lost her appetite.

Sam tried to remain stoic, but his bottom lip quivered. "Can . . . can I go with you, Gil? You might need someone to help."

"No." I grinned at him. "I need you here, with Margaret. You two can keep things going while I'm away."

"Awww, Gil. Margaret doesn't need me. Why, she's as good a cowboy as I ever seen. She can do just about anything."

Margaret blushed.

I nodded at her. "I know. And she's a jim-dandy with a rope, but I need you here, Sam. You understand?"

He nodded, disappointed.

"I'm just going to take a look. It might not be as bad as I've said. There might not be any snakes there at all. I've seen them, but it's been five years or so since I been through here. All I'm saying is that we might have some problems, but until we know for certain, let's don't worry too much."

Margaret swallowed hard and tugged her hat down on her head. "Isn't that a little like standing in the middle of the prairie with a stampede heading your way?"

With a sheepish grin, I replied. "I reckon. But you can't tell. Something might come along to turn the stampede."

"Yeah," she replied with a wry grin. "And something might not come along."

I reached the West Fork in midafternoon. To my surprise, the river was dry, its banks and bed cracked and parched. I reined up and stared at the dry riverbed. "What the blazes you figure happened here, Ned?'' I muttered softly, talking more to hear my own voice in the over-powering silence of the hill country.

Not that I objected. This way, we didn't have the water moccasins to worry about, but where in Sam Hill did the river go? Rivers just don't up and vanish. They're in particular places for particular reasons, and unless there was a mighty big change across the country, a river like the West Fork wasn't just going to hide behind the nearest tree.

Clicking my tongue, I sent Ned trotting across the bed, keeping my eyes peeled when I neared the far bank. The snakes could still be around. I doubted it, but I wasn't about to take any chances, none at all.

A few hundred yards beyond the dry bed, I found my answer.

A new river, this one with rocky banks and a gravel bed, twice the width of the old bed.

''Come on, Ned. Let's see what's going on here.'' I turned him north, upriver, watching the banks carefully for any sign of water moccasins.

Two miles up, I found a cave-in, one wall of a rocky bluff had fallen, blocking the old stream and forcing the water to carve out a new course. I retraced my trail, not once spotting a moccasin. I did disturb a nest of grass snakes, but the tiny fellers went skittering into the grass like green blurs.

Riding on downriver, I discovered where the new bed intersected the old one, and there I found the snakes, huge nests of black moccasins, their throats white as cotton balls, their fangs dripping with poison.

Their smell permeated the humid countryside, a musty, cloying odor that clung like a coat of thick mud, almost suffocating. When they spotted Ned and me, instantly they coiled, ready and anxious to fight.

"Come on, fella. Let's you and me head back. Leave these critters to themselves."

Far above the moccasins in the colder, faster water, we pushed the goats across the West Fork of the Nueces without incident, taking our time, giving the critters their fill of cold, sweet water. Up above the herd, we filled our canteens, gladly dumping the tepid water taken on back at Dry Devil's Creek.

Although we still had an hour of daylight after the crossing, we decided to camp on the riverbank that night, enjoy a cold bath in clean water, grab a little extra rest, and put away a meal of something other than beans and coffee.

To the east, we spotted Indian Mountain, only a couple thousand feet, but beyond it lay Black Mountain, Kelly Peak, Boiling Mountain, and Military Mountain, all rugged, choked with scrub forest and understory vegetation.

"We move northeast here," I announced later that night, sipping six-shooter coffee and chewing on some rabbit roasted too long over the fire. "It'll save us time in the long run." Nodding back to the east, I added, "Best I recollect, we've got over thirty miles of mountains thataway. Probably take two weeks to make it through. But, if we head back to the northeast, we can reach the main fork of the Nueces in two, three days, then head downriver to the East Fork. That oughta take another four days or so. That'll put us due east of San Antone in a week or so."

Chapter Sixteen

The three days to the Nueces were rugged, stumbling up and down rocky ravines, pushing through dense tangles of understory shrubbery, and blundering into box canyons.

But at the close of the third day, we burst out of the shrub forest onto a grassy plain in the middle of which flowed the Nueces River, its banks lined with drooping willows and shaded by tall cottonwoods.

I rode ahead, searching the fast-moving water for snakes, but I failed to spot any. With a sign of relief, I reined Ned around and waited for Shoelink to lead the herd in.

Sam pulled up beside me and nodded to the river. ''Any snakes?''

''None. Water's fast and pretty clear. Most water moccasins prefer slower water, sluggish . . . like a backwater swamp or slough.''

I started to say more, but decided to keep my mouth shut.

Sam said it for me. ''What about farther down? Where this river runs into the West Fork?''

I glanced at Shoelink and Margaret before replying, then shrugged. ''Probably.''

The young man stared levelly at me, then nodded. ''Oh.''

For several seconds, no one spoke, each thinking about what lay ahead. I broke the silence. ''I don't know about the rest of you, but I'm tired of beans.'' I grinned at Sam and hooked my thumb at the river. ''How about some fresh-caught fish? In the clear water, they oughta be sweet-tasting.''

"Yeah." Sam grinned from ear to ear. "Let's catch some fish.''

Shoelink built a fire while the three of us found branches and rigged up some crude fishing poles. We managed to scrounge up a couple of safety pins for Margaret and Sam. I whittled a hook out of an oak branch for me. We dug in the muddy banks and came up with fat worms that wriggled and twisted on the hooks like a tangle of string.

"Boy howdy," Sam exclaimed as he dropped his line into the water. "The way that worm's wiggling, oughta get me a nice fat fish.''

Before anyone could reply, a fish hit the worm and almost jerked the branch from Sam's hands. He yanked hard. The pole bent, then snapped back, and a broken line dangled from the end.

"Wow." Sam whistled. "Did you see that, Gil?''

"I sure did, boy." I handed him my pole. "Here. Use this one while I rig up another.''

Excited by the fish he had lost, Sam grabbed my pole and dangled another wiggling worm in the water. Before he could catch a breath, Margaret shouted and heaved a fat catfish from the water.

The twisting fish snapped its mouth off the hook and splashed back in the water. Then Sam yelled and yanked, but all he came up with was a broken oak hook. He looked at me in disappointment.

Shoelink shuffled up, eyed the broken gear, shook his head, then said. "Zhou Gui Ling get fish." He held up his finger as if to warn us. "Must be quiet. No noise, no sound." He shook his head.

Without another word, he waded into the river and paused in knee-deep water. He bent at the waist and lowered his arms into the water. He remained motionless as a tree stump for several seconds, and then, effortlessly, slowly, he rose without wrinkling the water, holding a fat catfish by the bottom lip.

With a flick of his wrist, he tossed the fish to the bank and then bent over once again. Margaret looked at me in disbelief. Sam muttered, ''Wow.''

Moments later, Shoelink came up with another catfish. He paused, holding the twisting fish by his side. He nodded to the first fish, still flopping on the ground. ''Eat. Fire.'' And then he tossed us the second catfish.

With a chuckle, I wasted no time gutting, then skinning the catfish. Sam cut some green branches for spits, and within a few minutes, the white flesh of the catfish crackled from the heat.

Shoelink stopped after the fifth catfish, but there's no question in my mind that the little Oriental could have kept yanking catfish from the water as long as he wanted, or as long as they lasted.

Later that night, after Margaret and Sam had dropped off to sleep, I asked Shoelink how he had learned to catch fish in such a manner. He gazed into the fire, and for a brief, flickering moment, his eyes glazed over as he returned to his youth in that small, strange country on the other side of the world.

''Venerable grandfather,'' he whispered. ''He was a . . .'' He searched for the word, pantomiming chopping with a hoe. He wrinkled his brow with a frown. ''How you say . . . ?''

''Farmer? Farming?''

He nodded emphatically. ''Ai. Far-ming. He live by a little river.'' He gestured to the Nueces and shook his head. ''This much, much more river than honorable grandfather.

He catch fish, much fish. Sings to them. Holds food for them.''

I sat back and eyed him skeptically. ''Sings to them?''

''Ai. Little song.'' And then in his frail, sing-song voice, he broke into one of the strangest languages I had ever heard. Chinese, I guessed.

When he finished, I asked, ''What was the song about?''

He smiled, a dreamy smile that seemed to say he was still back in the land of his memories. ''Ah, song is to little fish, telling them my wife, my child be sick. The fish must come to my hand to make my family not sick no more.''

I leaned back against my saddle and cupped the mug of steaming coffee in my hands. Remembering pieces of my own short childhood, I stared at him silently as he continued to gaze into space. Other than the color of our skin, Shoelink and me were just alike.

During the night, a wolf howled, but the cry was distant and came no closer. I lay awake, listening. I heard Sam cough. When I looked, the boy was awake, his Winchester lying across his chest.

The boy was quickly becoming a young man. I rolled over and promptly went back to sleep.

We pushed south the next morning, staying on the grassy plain that paralleled the river, making our journey easy, almost lazy. We had our fill of fish the next few days, and it wasn't until we were ready to gag at the sight of fish that I brought us in some venison, a nice fat one.

With the skillet piping hot, I dropped in some venison fat, which quickly melted. When the grease started bubbling, I plopped in a thick steak that fried quickly, which was the secret of tasty venison.

Venison has little fat, and none of the marbled steaks

that come from standard cuts of beef. If a jasper leaves venison in the skillet too long, he'll have himself a slab of meat that would do good service as boot leather.

So, pop it in, pop it out. A minute, no more than two on each side and you have a delicious strip of venison.

The last night before we reached the fork, we filled our stomachs with venison. Sam licked his lips and dragged his sleeve across his mouth to clean off the grease. "That sure is good, Gil."

I winked at Margaret, who was holding her own with the venison. I had to hand it to her. When we started, I figured her for a complainer, a pain in the neck, but she had been neither. Oh, she'd fussed, but we'd all fussed, about the weather, the wolves, any of the hundred other discomforts that are part of a cattle drive—a goat drive, I should say. She was a good hand, and from where I came from, you couldn't pay a man or a woman a bigger compliment.

She smiled back. "It is good. Tender. Usually, deer is tough, but this melts in your mouth."

Their compliments put me in an expansive mood. "Let me tell you about some venison I had one year, near Christmas. Me and Shoshone Pete, he was a cantankerous old mountain man on his last legs . . . I was about fifteen or so, and well, we was up in the mountains, living in an old tree that was rotted out on the inside. With our fire, we was as snug as you could imagine—Indian blanket over the opening to keep out the cold. Well, Pete took a haunch of venison, stuffed it with all sorts of tasty herbs and spices he dug up from the forest, added a bunch of crushed hickory and pecan nuts, some dried apples, then coated it with wild honey inside and out and baked it in a rock oven he'd built next to the fire."

Sam's tongue darted out and licked his lips.

"To go with the roast, we had fresh sourdough biscuits, a bowl of Indian succotash, and a juicy pudding out of wild plums." I leaned back and patted my stomach. "Yes, sir, that was the best Christmas I reckon I ever spent, just me and Pete holed up in that big old hollow tree with the snow coming down outside like the heavens had opened up and forgot to close back."

Margaret glanced up at me, the firelight dancing off the dimples in her cheeks. "Where were you and Pete?"

The firelight dancing across her face made her eyes impossible to read. I couldn't tell if the question was simply a polite one, or if she was really interested. Strangely enough, I found I was hoping for the latter. "Up in Wyoming. In the Tetons, north of Jackson Hole. That's where my ranch is . . . at least, the one I want to buy into."

The grin faded from Sam's face. "I . . . I was hoping you'd changed your mind, Gil. I mean, about staying down here. Pa's ranch is awful big . . . too big for me."

I tried not to grimace. I was becoming attached to the boy. He was hard-working, and he listened, but I had a life of my own. The ranch in the Tetons was my last chance to make something of myself. I'd seen many a drifter planted in the ground without even a regret or a tear shed for them. The next day, he was a forgotten man. No one remembered his name.

No. I wasn't too religious, but I believed in God. This beautiful country just couldn't have happened, and people couldn't have just come out of thin air. A Hand smarter and wiser than mine did it, and I always figured He had plans for us to be something more than just line-riding cowpokes.

Sam continued when I didn't immediately reply. "You could have part of the ranch, Gil. I'd give it to you. That way, it would be your own."

His sincerity touched me. I leaned forward and ruffled his hair. "Thanks, Sam, that's mighty generous, but your pa worked too hard for you to just up and give part of his ranch away."

Margaret leaned over and laid her hand on Sam's arm.

He forced a weak smile.

"You're a growing young man, Sam," she said. "Before long, you'll be able to run everything yourself."

His shoulders sagged. "How long will that be? I'm only thirteen. Another two or three years? Besides, you know how grown-ups treat kids."

Margaret shot me an icy look. "Things will work out, Sam. Don't worry."

I glanced at Shoelink, but the slightly built Oriental man turned his back to the fire and pulled the blanket over his shoulder. I had the distinct feeling that he was trying to tell me something, and there was no question in my mind what that something was.

Chapter Seventeen

We reached the confluence of the Nueces and the West Fork of the Nueces two days later. The water grew shallow as the river widened, pushing the muddy banks apart until the width of the river was almost twice that of the head-waters five days earlier.

The next morning, I rode ahead, instructing the others to keep the herd in place until I returned.

I searched for a ford, a broad and shallow crossing, constantly watching for cottonmouths. I spotted one or two, nothing out of the ordinary. "Hold on there, Ned," I muttered, reining up and staring ahead at a ford that looked like it had been put there just for us.

A broad, rocky bank, at least a hundred yards wide, sloped to the river. On either side were banks several feet high, the bases of which were choked with thickets, ideal habitats for the cottonmouth. But in between was only the sloping rock. The far shore was identical, like a giant glacier centuries past had slid into the river on one side and out the other.

Taking care, I urged Ned into the water. My grin broadened as the water remained about his fetlocks. Upon reaching the far side, I turned and shook my head. "Don't that beat the tarnation? It was right here waiting for us, Ned." I eyed the ford in wonder. "I just can't believe it. Ain't that the luck?"

Ned whinnied and shook his head. I gave a click of my tongue. "Come on, feller. Let's get us back."

"No snakes. Not like before," I repeated to Margaret. "I spotted maybe one or two along the way, but that's normal. The ford is perfect."

Sam rode drag, about half a mile back. The goats continued on their slow, steady course behind the bell goat and Shoelink, who bounced from one foot to the other, singing in his funny little voice to the goats.

I couldn't help thinking about Sam's profits from the herd. With careful handling, and hard work, he could build him a nice spread back out there at Painted Comanche Tree. I glanced sidelong at Margaret, then quickly looked away, trying not to wonder about what would happen to her.

And to Shoelink. I knew he felt a deep obligation to me, but surely he didn't figure the debt meant a trip to Wyoming and the Tetons.

Then I had an idea. A perfect solution. Shoelink could stay with Sam. The little Chinese fella needed a home, and Sam needed help. A perfect solution.

We hit the fork in the rivers just after lunch, and immediately pushed the herd into the water. By now, they offered no resistance, simply followed the critters ahead of them.

With Margaret on the downstream side of the herd and me on the upstream side, we acted as flankers to keep the herd in line as it forded the river. I kept my eyes moving, watching the oncoming waters, searching for the telltale black shadow of any cottonmouth drawn to the commotion created by the critters.

But the herd made little disturbance.

We didn't see our first snake until the herd was almost

over, and then suddenly, near the bank behind us, a tiny kid bleated and bounced out of the water and across the river like a rubber ball.

Behind, several rams wheeled about and tore the shallow water into a mixture of mud and foam. Moments later, the muddy water took on a red tinge.

"Look," shouted Margaret, pointing at the dead snake floating downriver.

Before I could reply, half a dozen rams churned another corner of the ford into a froth.

I grinned at Margaret. "Maybe we didn't need to worry about these critters after all."

She shook her head. "I knew hogs killed snakes, but I didn't figure goats did too."

"Beats me." I wheeled Ned back toward the far shore. "I never heard of goats taking after snakes, but then I never had anything to do with goats until seven months ago. For all I know, they can do back flips."

Margaret chuckled, her dimpled cheeks rosy. "They might be able to do a lot of things, but I doubt if back flips are one of them."

I arched an eyebrow. "Want to bet?"

Thirty minutes later, the last goat waded out of the river and hurried after the herd disappearing into the mesquite and juniper.

We cut due east, maybe five days from our destination. We still had the Frio, the Hondo, and the Medina Rivers to cross, but the two forks of the Nueces were the ones I had worried most about, the ones I'd heard most of the stories about.

The terrain began rolling, cut by rocky arroyos and gullies, both shallow and deep. As we slipped and slid down one and scrabbled up the far side, Sam shouted, "Look! Over there, a cave."

Sure enough, down the gully, the mouth of a cave gaped, a dark hole in the middle of the white limestone. "Boy," he gushed, "it'd sure be fun to explore it."

"Yeah." I winked at Margaret. "Be fun dancing around all the snakes and centipedes you'd find inside. Besides, you remember our last cave."

He shivered and wrinkled his nose. "Centipedes. You mean 'hundred legs?'"

I nodded, glancing around to make sure the critters were still trailing.

"I wouldn't like that."

"Oh, no?" I grinned, figuring on having a little fun with Sam. "Not even for a hundred thousand dollars?"

His eyes bugged out. "A hundred thousand dollars?"

"Yep." I nodded, deliberately saying no more.

He looked at Margaret, who shrugged, then turned back to me. "Where is it? Where is that much money?"

I glanced at the sun. We had about two hours before sundown. "Tell you what, soon as we get the herd bedded, I'll tell you the story. It's about Jim Bowie . . ."

Sam interrupted. "The same Jim Bowie that helped make Texas a republic? Huh?"

"Yeah. Hey, you remembered."

He grinned. "I'm not just a dumb kid all the time. I like the idea of a republic too."

My chest swelled with pride. That was one of the first times anyone had taken something I'd said and made it a part of them, kind of like when a jasper goes to Sunday meeting and takes home some of the things the parson spouts.

That's how I felt. A new strength that was exciting, but also scary. What if I told the boy something that hurt him?

Suddenly, I realized this ma-pa business was a mighty serious undertaking. Like building a cabin, but not having the chance to go back and correct a door that you hung wrong. I'd heard an old carpenter once say, "Measure twice, cut once, but if it's wrong, throw it away and start over."

That sure wouldn't work here. You can't throw a child away and start over. Yes, sir, those Tetons were looking mighty good to me.

Sam's rapid-fire questions interrupted my own thoughts. I put him off. "Tonight, okay? Let's get settled in, and then I'll tell you all about Jim Bowie's silver up along the Frio."

"The Frio?" Sam was irrepressible. "Where's the Frio, Gil? Huh? Around here somewhere? Huh?"

I held up my hand. "Tonight, boy. Tonight. Now, you get back to drag. We still got a couple hours."

"Yes, sir. Don't worry about me." He wheeled his pony about and skittered back through the juniper and mesquite.

Margaret pulled up beside me and laughed. "I think you created yourself a monster."

I laughed with her. "You mean, about the silver and caves?"

"Yes."

Briefly, I remembered my own pa and some of the outrageous windies he told me, not deliberate lies, but stretchers. Often I dropped off to sleep thinking of ghosts and goblins, boogeymen and rawhead and bloody bones.

"Boys enjoy that sort of thing," I replied. "At least, I did. You figure, a trail drive is a long ways from a box supper. The boy needs something to take his mind off the dust he'll be eating come tomorrow."

Margaret didn't reply at once. She just stared at me with a funny, puzzled look. Finally, she said. "I wish you'd reconsider that ranch up in the Tetons."

I frowned, thinking I had misunderstood her, but then I

realized that I had heard her clearly. Couldn't she understand how important that ranch was for me?

Before I could reply, she added. "You would be a wonderful father for Sam."

All I could do was stare at her, my jaw agape like a
poleaxed steer ready to crumple to his knees. "W . . .
What?"

"I know you've never given it any thought, but he truly
admires you, and he will need help on the ranch."

She paused, waiting for me to reply, but I'm one of those
who always thinks of the right thing to say too late, and
this time, her proposal was so crazy and outlandish that all
I could do was stutter.

She saw that her remarks had overwhelmed me, so she
smiled primly and said. "You don't have to decide right
away, but it is something you should think about. Sam's a
good boy."

By now, I'd collected my thoughts, and she was right.
Her remark had overwhelmed me, but not the way she
thought. She thought I took it as a compliment, but as far
as I was concerned, she just thought I was stupid enough
to give up everything of which I had dreamed for the boy.

I shook my head emphatically. "No, Ma'am. No way
I'm staying down here. True enough, I like the boy . . . a
whole lot, but what happens when he becomes full-grown?
He's got his place, and I got nothing. Now, you might think
that's selfish on my part, but then, you got a pa who built
you a nice spread, and from everything I've seen in knocking about the country, it's a heap easier to give advice when
you don't have as much to lose."

Her cheeks colored as if I'd slapped her. "But . . ."

I wheeled Ned around. "No buts. No talk. I got one last
chance to build something for me and a family whenever
I get one. I don't plan on letting nothing stop me."

* * *

Margaret was sullen and quiet that night, which was just fine with me. I'd had my fill of someone trying to tell me what I wanted to do, especially someone who had everything handed to her, and who knew nothing about life and the hard knocks it dished out.

We had run across a small glade at the junction of several rocky canyons, in which the critters could meander without much danger of drifting away. We camped under an old mesquite, the trunk of which was about a yard thick and eight to ten feet around. Huge limbs forked from the trunk, providing a patchy canopy over our heads.

Sam filled his plate, then squatted cross-legged beside me. "Okay, Gil. Now, what about Jim Bowie's cave and all the silver?"

I poured another cup of coffee and leaned back against my saddle. Margaret was staring into the fire while Shoelink sat scratching Mutt, who was sleeping the sleep of the dead beside the fire.

"Well, it was years back, maybe forty ... forty-five, somewhere in the early '30s, and Jim and a band of filibusters was heading northwest out of San Antone."

Sam frowned. "What are filibusters, huh, Gil?"

I thought a moment. "Explorers, I reckon you could say. Men who travel around the country trying to explore some way to make them rich."

"Like gold miners?"

"Not exactly. Filibusters were more like mercenaries, men who fought for the country that paid them the most money."

Sam interrupted. "Why ... ?"

"Hold it, boy." It was my turn to interrupt him. "You want to hear the story or ask foolish questions?"

Sam clamped his lips shut. Then, in a voice squeaky as a mouse, he whispered, "The story."

I nodded with finality. "Okay, so, like I was saying, Jim and his boys moved out of San Antone until they hit the Frio River. Story was, they were heading to El Paso to fight for the Mexican army. I don't know if that's true or not, but anyway, the spot they hit on the Frio was about two, three days northwest of San Antone. Someone, maybe Bowie himself, stumbled on a vein of silver, so they forgot about the filibustering and started digging. While some of the men dug, others built a rock fort just in case they had trouble with the Comanches. They must have dug down forty or fifty feet before the Comanches hit."

Sam's eyes grew wide.

"Yep. Well, a royal battle took place, two, three days, until Bowie's water ran low."

"Why'd the Comanche attack him?"

I shrugged. "Who knows? Maybe Jim and his boys had trespassed onto Comanche land. If that was true, they could have probably worked out some compromise, but the story is, one of Jim's boys got off the first shot and killed the chief's son."

After taking a sip of coffee, I continued. "Anyway, some of the filibusters fought from the rock fort while the others buried their silver in the cave, enough treasure, the story goes, to lay a road of silver from Painted Comanche Tree to San Antone."

Shoelink looked up from scratching Mutt and arched an eyebrow. I grinned sheepishly, for I had been stretching the story some, but it made for interesting listening to the boy. "Pure silver, piles of it. More silver than you could shake a stick at. Anyway, they fought for days, then Jim and what was left of his bunch managed to slip out one night and escape. They made it back to San Antone, where they spread the story of the silver.''

Sam whistled soundlessly. ''They go back and get the silver?''

I shrugged and poured some more coffee and tried to appear nonchalant. ''Some went back, but none ever got the silver. It was lost. Jim went back, but he couldn't find the right place.''

''You mean . . .'' Sam's eyes grew as big as two tin plates. ''You mean, the silver is still up there?''

Keeping a straight face, I nodded soberly. ''Yep. Even today, and many a jasper has tried to find it.''

''And never did?''

''And never did.''

''Why? You think it was the Indians what kept them from finding the silver?''

''Might have been, but if it was, they had a reason. I never met an Injun that wasn't reasonable. Now sometimes, an Injun's reasonable isn't anything like my reasonable or your reasonable, but then, I suppose that's to be expected when you got two hombres from two different cultures trying to work out something.''

Sam's forehead wrinkled as he considered my explanation. ''Yeah. I see how that can be. Kinda like a dog and cat trying to drink from the same bowl, huh?''

I chuckled. ''I reckon.'' The boy was a mighty fast study.

''What was the Indians really like, Gil? Back in New Jersey, we heard all kinds of terrible things.''

''I reckon that was stretched some, boy. I been up and down the river a few times and met many an Injun. Never had one break his word to me, and while I never had any sidekicks other than old Shoelink here, I've seen a heap of Injuns I'd partner with over many a white man any day.''

"You mean, they don't kill like I hear?"

"Some do. Some don't. Same as the white man. I've never killed an hombre. Shot up a bunch, but to the best of my knowledge, I never killed one, but there's many a white man who can't say that. You see, boy, we're all the same, just different color skins, different religions, different habits, but down deep, we're all the same."

Sam cut his eyes at Shoelink, then grinned at me. "Yeah. I see what you mean." He shook his head. "And you think the silver is still there, huh?"

"Can't say for sure, but tomorrow we hit the Frio."

Sam's eyes bugged out. "We do what?" He stared at me, not really certain he understood what I was saying.

"That's right. We hit the Frio, the river the silver mine is by." I hooked my thumb over my shoulder. "About three days upstream."

His enthusiasm boiled over. "Let's go, Gil. Let's go find the silver." He bounced up and down.

"What about your goats, boy? What do you do with them?"

The excitement on his face faded. "Oh, yeah. I forgot. We got to take the goats on to San Antonio." His face lit up as an idea struck. "But we can go up there on the way home, huh? There ain't no Indians now."

I laughed and glanced at Margaret, who gave no indication of hearing us. One thing she had been right about, I'd created me a little monster. "We'll see, boy, we'll see."

Chapter Eighteen

The campfire burned low while Sam and I talked. The shadows flickering on the canopy of mesquite leaves overhead grew smaller and slower. Margaret had long since climbed into her soogan and pulled the tarp up over her head, which was fine with me.

As if on cue, Mutt looked up at me. I nodded, and he rose and hobbled into the night to watch the herd. I followed moments later.

"I'll come out about two, Gil," said Sam from the camp as I rode out.

I chuckled. "I'll be waiting."

Usually when I nighthawked, I whistled or sang to help pass the time. With beeves, a man's voice calmed them. With goats, I had no idea, but since they didn't stampede when I sang, I figured there was no harm in it.

But tonight, I didn't sing. Margaret's remarks stayed in my head despite my efforts to push them aside. They were like a large carbuncle that kept growing and growing until finally you had to take a hot bottle and stick the mouth over the sore. When the bottle cooled, it burst the sore, pulling out all the poison and infection.

There was no way I could get rid of my carbuncle. I didn't have the right kind of hot bottle to pop it. Try as I might, I couldn't get her remarks off my mind. I repeated my plans, my goals. I spoke of them aloud to Ned and the goats. In the still night air, they sounded exalted, lofty, almost noble, the goals every man should set for himself.

So why did I feel so guilty about them?

When Sam relieved me at two, I hurried back to camp and slipped into my blankets, hoping for the emptiness of sleep to wipe away the questions tumbling about my head.

But sleep didn't come. I lay awake and watched the Big Dipper march about the North Star. Three o'clock, then four.

Disgusted, I threw back my blanket and stuck some wood on the fire. If I couldn't sleep, then I'd at least drink me some coffee.

Suddenly, the thud of hooves broke the silence. I looked up to see Sam come flying into camp. I grabbed my handgun.

"Gil. Come quick. I heard something."

The others sat up.

"What are you talking about, boy?"

He held his pony in place. "Somebody's out there, Gil. I heard somebody crying."

I slipped my six-gun back in the holster. "Probably a coyote or something."

"No. Honest. It sounded like a person."

Margaret laid her hand on my arm. "Could it be a person?"

"No." I shook my head. "Out here? Why would anybody be out here?"

Sam reined the pony around. "That direction." He pointed north. "It sounded like someone crying."

I looked down at Margaret, then glanced across the fire at Shoelink, who arched a questioning eyebrow. I knew nothing would do but that I go out and see what was bothering Sam. If it wasn't a coyote, it was probably two limbs rubbing against each other in the wind. Strange things happened out in the wilderness, especially at night, when a jasper's imagination got all stirred up.

"You two stay here. We'll call if we need you." And Sam and me rode out with Mutt at our heels.

The stars overhead were a solid bowl of diamonds, lighting our path even without the moon. From horizon to horizon, stars twinkled and danced, making a jasper feel right small.

Back to the south, a flash of orange appeared over the treetops. Several seconds later, the ominous roll of thunder rumbled across the countryside. I grimaced, remembering the last time the rain came.

Sam reined up. "Right here," he whispered, holding up his hand.

I listened.

Crickets chirruped. An owl hooted, and the startled hustle of a frightened animal rustled the underbrush. But no cries.

Minutes passed.

Sam shifted around in the saddle nervously. Finally, he looked up at me, his eyebrows knitted. "Honest, Gil. I heard it. I promise."

I didn't want to embarrass the boy. I knew he'd heard something. His imagination just got the best of him. Happened a lot at night by yourself.

"Well, son, whatever it was, it ain't there now. Why don't you go on back. I'm awake now."

"But . . . that isn't fair . . . to you I mean. I only been out here a couple hours. It's still two hours till daylight."

"Don't worry about it. Tell you what. You can go back and bring me a cup of coffee. I never did get one."

Even in the starlight, I could see the grin leap to his face. "Yes, sir. Be right back."

I watched the younker disappear into the night. He was a good kid, and if I had a mind to raise a youngster, I could do a lot worse than him. But I didn't have time. I was twenty-seven, going on twenty-eight. I had a heap of work to do before I could even start to think about raising youngsters.

To the south, another roll of thunder reverberated through the still air, seeming to shake the ground at my feet. Suddenly, I stiffened. Mixed with the rumbling of the approaching storm was another sound, faint, distant—as unintelligible to my ears as the bubbling of a baby.

What was it? A cry?

Standing at Ned's feet, Mutt stared into the night, his ears perked forward.

I cocked my head and turned my ear into the wind and listened hard. All I heard was the ghostly moan of the wind, intensifying with each breath. The storm rolled nearer, its dark clouds erupting with explosions of orange, followed seconds later by blasts of thunder.

The goats stirred nervously, gathering under the junipers and mesquites, backing up to the walls of the rocky canyons surrounding us.

Mutt peered first in one direction, then another, trying to pinpoint whatever we heard.

I strained to hear, but there was nothing except the blowing wind and rolling thunder and approaching lightning. Sitting back in my saddle, I muttered. ''Blasted imagination, Ned. Nights like this, it'll drive a man to cuss. Why . . .''

Then I heard it again. Behind me, in the canyon.

I wheeled Ned around and stared into the night, squinting hard into the darkness as if straining my eyes would help me hear better.

A growl sounded in Mutt's throat.

A gust of wind slammed into my back, sent dry leaves skittering noisily over the ground. I muttered a curse and waited for the next break in the wind.

The wind settled. I heard nothing. But I remembered some of the Indian tales about wandering spirits and haunts. ''Get ahold of yourself, Gil,'' I muttered. ''No such things as goblins and ghosts.''

Mutt continued to growl.

For several moments, I continued staring into the darkness of the canyon. There was something out there. I had heard it. And it wasn't no ghost. Slowly, I eased the rawhide loop off the hammer of my six-gun and urged Ned toward the mouth of the canyon.

While the goats had nervously bunched in preparation for the storm, they did not seem particularly jittery, which they would have had there been coyotes or wolves around.

With Mutt at our side, Ned and me eased through the herd until we reached the mouth of the canyon. I reined up and listened. Like a living thing, the wind was caught up in the crosscurrents of the canyon, moaning and sighing, howling and wailing, coming and going from every direction. Its hand slapped my face, and in the next moment, clapped me on the back. Its fingers tugged my shirtsleeves and then yanked my vest.

I pulled my hat down over my eyes.

The next several seconds, only the wind filled my ears with its plaintive moans. Just as I started to rein Ned around, I heard the sound again, this time just after the wind laid.

A cry. It was a cry.

Instantly, I grew tense, shucking my .44 and peering in the direction of the cry. I discounted an ambush. Not in a box canyon with the wall at their back. But I was taking no chances. ''Easy, Ned.''

Mutt continued to growl.

The canyon walls grew higher the farther I rode into the canyon. I reined up, puzzled. I'd heard nothing for the last few minutes. Had it all just been my imagination? Was it the convoluted and labyrinthine funnels of wind distorted by the fissures and clefts in the rocky walls? Or had I really heard the cry?

I looked at Mutt. His ears were laid back, and the growls sounded deep in his throat.

Then I heard it again, this time along the canyon wall to my right. Mutt barked. ''Shut up,'' I snapped, at the same time urging Ned in the direction of the sound. Every muscle in my body strained to the point of breaking. Slowly, I eased back the hammer on my .44. Whatever was out there was only a hairbreadth away from a hundred-and-eighty-five-grain chunk of lead.

Along the wall, the juniper grew thick and dense.

The sound grew louder, clearer, a high-pitched moan.

Mutt stayed beside Ned, growls continually rolling from deep in his throat.

Suddenly, behind the junipers, a dark opening appeared in the canyon wall. The moans seemed to be coming from that direction.

I pulled Ned up and shouted at the cave. ''Who's there?''

The moans ceased.

''You heard me. Who's in there? I don't mean any harm.''

A faint, desperate voice crackled. ''Please. Help me. Help me.''

Mutt stopped growling.

I glanced at him, then back at the cave. ''Who are you? Who's in there?'' I wasn't taking any chances.

''Please . . . Please, help me. I . . .''

The wind whipped the last words away, and a crack of

lightning blasted the canyon with a blinding flash of white light.

A wall of rain struck, soaking me instantly.

Quickly, I dismounted and knelt behind a juniper. I kept my eyes on the cave. It was dark. I flexed my fingers on my .44. Beside me, Mutt whined and wagged his tail. Before I could stop him, he limped through the junipers to the cave.

"Mutt! Get back here."

He ignored me and disappeared into the cave. Moments later, he barked, and a voice said, "Nice puppy . . . Nice puppy."

Overhead, rain fell in torrents. Lightning crashed and exploded. Without waiting, I dashed to the face of the canyon and pressed myself against the rocky wall next to the mouth of the cave.

A frail voice drifted from the darkness. "Please . . . help."

Mutt came back out, barked once at me, then hopped back inside. I followed.

Just inside the mouth, I froze as the lightning revealed a thin woman lying on the cave floor. Holstering my six-gun, I knelt at her side and gently lifted her, noticing instantly that she was with child. "Who are you?" I whispered. "Where's your husband?"

"I . . . He's . . ." She went limp in my arms. Quickly, I felt her pulse. It was steady. But she was cold and shivering. I had to get her warm.

I shook my head. Gil Vince, caretaker of lost dogs, lost boys, lost women, lost Orientals, lost goats, lost everything. Would it ever end?

I sighed and laid her back gently, then removed my soogan from behind the cantle of my saddle and managed to get her in it. Once I got her covered up to her neck, I set about trying to build a fire.

Despite the rain, I managed to find enough dead wood to coax up a small flame, the heat of which quickly dried the wet logs and then consumed them.

I looked around the cave. Mutt lay by the fire while Ned stood hipshot just inside the cave, out of the rain. I chuckled. ''Don't blame you boys.'' I looked down at the woman. She was unconscious, but at least she was warm.

What she needed was a woman's touch.

Rising quickly, I led Ned outside and mounted. ''Come on, boy. Let's get back to camp.''

The spreading mesquite under which we had camped did nothing to keep the rain off. The camp was a miserable sight, all three rolled up in their soogans around the black ashes of a dead fire.

I roused them, and ten minutes later, we three men were squatting around the warm fire while Margaret looked after the unconscious woman. Outside, the rain continued.

''I remember last time we was in a cave and it rained, don't you, Gil?'' Sam had a worried look on his face.

''Yeah, boy, but I reckon this is a little different, huh, Shoelink?''

The small Oriental looked up from where he was rubbing his hands together over the fire and grunted. ''Ai.'' He touched his head. ''Man no sense in this weather. Should be by fire, like us.''

Margaret looked around. ''She's okay, just weak. We need to get her some soup.''

I frowned. ''Soup? Where are we going to get soup?''

Shoelink rose quickly. ''I fix. Much, much good for little lady.''

''How?'' I shook my head. ''We don't have a pot.''

He shrugged. "Zhou Gui Ling show *Sangsu*." He pulled out a tin plate, set it on a rock by the fire, and filled it with water, after which he crushed two handfuls of beans and dropped them into the water. As the mixture came to a boil, he dumped several herbs and spices in it.

Within minutes, a delicious aroma filled the cave. My mouth watered, Sam's mouth watered, and Mutt started wagging his tail. Margaret shook her head and squatted by the fire, stirring the soup. "Don't even think about it, boys. This soup is for the lady. She needs her strength. I think she is just about ready to have a baby."

Well, that little announcement did away with my appetite in no uncertain terms. "A baby?" I looked around frantically. "Out here? She can't. She's got to wait. Have her wait."

Margaret arched an eyebrow. "I have news for you, Gil Vince. You might know about herding goats and cattle, but you don't know nothing about babies. Babies don't wait." Using her bandanna to keep from burning her fingers, she carried the soup to the woman and gently fed her.

I plopped down beside the fire and reached for the coffeepot with shaking hands. A baby. Out here in the middle of the wilderness—with two thousand or more goats, three horses, and a burro. That just didn't make any sense at all.

Margaret's words suddenly broke the silence, a short, terse exclamation. "Uh-oh."

I froze. "Uh-oh? Did you say uh-oh?"

Chapter Nineteen

Instantly, the tension in the cave grew tighter than a fresh-shrunk rim on a wagon wheel.

Margaret ignored my question. "Shoelink, I need some hot water. Now," she said.

His eyes twinkled. "Yes, Missy. Hot water. Soon." He nodded to the fire, where another pan of water was beginning to boil.

The rain continued, but the storm was passing, for the lightning and thunder had moved on north. Outside, the sky grew lighter. I rose and slipped on my slicker. "Come on, Sam, let's you and me check on the herd. Looks like we're going to be stuck here a day or two."

Heads down, backs into the rain, the herd stood disconsolately among the juniper and against the canyon walls, soaked to the skin. We rode through them, then around the perimeter. They had barely moved during the night, but now, with the storm passing, they'd be anxious to find browse for their bellies.

We could let them drift and browse, but not far, no more than a mile or so in any direction. With luck, maybe we could move out tomorrow.

I pondered over the woman and her situation as we rode. A woman in her condition had no reason to be out in the middle of Texas, miles from civilization. Besides, how did

153

she reach the cave? Where was her husband? What about their transportation?

The rain had been heavy, but there would have been some sign of wagon tracks.

"Something wrong, Gil?"

I looked down at Sam. "No, boy. Just puzzled. That's all."

"About the lady?"

"Yeah."

Sam didn't reply right away. He leaned over and patted his pony's neck. "You figure they were homesteaders?"

"Maybe. Maybe not. Oh, I'm sure they were heading someplace to settle. That's the only explanation for them being out here."

"You think she'll be okay?"

I hesitated, and looked back in the direction of the cave. "I reckon. Giving birth is a normal thing for women, boy. But just because it's normal doesn't mean it's easy. Takes a heap of grit and determination."

Sam gazed back toward the cave. Questions filled his head. "Is that why ma's look after their young'uns so much, because it was hard for them to get the kids?"

"Well, boy, I wouldn't exactly say it like that." I chuckled. "When the ma sees that child, there's a love that you can't take a measuring stick to. What you said is all mixed together with that love in her feelings. That child is the most important and valuable thing she has."

"More important than her husband?" A frown etched wrinkles in Sam's forehead.

"Reckon that'd be a toss-up. The feelings she has for each are mighty strong . . . not much different, I don't reckon. Fact is, I'd sure hate to have to live off that difference."

Sam nodded. "I think I understand. It's sort of like that with these mama goats and their kids, huh?"

I reined Ned up and looked down at the young man. He had me uncomfortable with all these questions, questions I'd never given much thought to. Now I was thinking and talking at the same time, which had never been one of my strong suits. So I took my time. I had the feeling that somehow what we were talking about was important. "Yeah, reckon so. Sort of. I reckon the good Lord gave all mamas feelings for their younkers. I've seen a mama wolf tear into a mountain lion that was after her cub. And sow bears, they don't cotton to no one messing with their little ones. So, to answer your question, yeah . . . all mamas look after their children, but the human mama just does it a heap longer, all of her life, in fact."

I paused, wondering if I'd made a complete fool of myself, halfway expecting Sam to burst out laughing. But he didn't. Instead, he regarded me seriously, nodded briefly, and replied, "I see."

We heard the baby squalling when we pulled up in front of the cave. Sam looked up and grinned like a possum. "It's a baby." He jumped from the saddle and hurried inside.

I leaned back against the cantle, and my shoulders sagged. What else could go wrong? We were still five days from San Antonio and now I had a mother and a new infant to consider. How were they going to travel?

I had my answer when Sam came bouncing back out of the cave, his arms and legs waving all out of kilter. He shouted, "It's a boy, Gil! It's a boy."

Anyone with as much energy as Sam could walk. I'd stick mother and child on Sam's pony, and Sam could tag along beside Shoelink. With a satisfied grin, I slipped out of the saddle and went inside to see the new baby.

Margaret nodded across the fire at me. "They're fine." Before I could open my mouth, she continued. "Her name is Rebecca . . . Rebecca Graham. She and her husband, Wardlow, were heading to San Antonio from El Paso. Their wagon broke down north of here, beyond the canyon. Her husband went out to find some food, but never returned. He took their only horse, so after a week, Rebecca started walking. She stopped in here for the night, but the next morning, her labor began."

I stared at her, amazed at how much she had learned while in the midst of delivering a baby.

Margaret shrugged and arched an eyebrow. "And you know the rest."

I groaned. Yeah, I knew the rest. How well I knew the rest. I glanced out the mouth of the cave. At least there was a wagon around. Might as well take a look at it.

Sam and I found the wagon, a Conestoga, about two hours north, busted down in the middle of a rocky canyon when the off rear wheel dropped into a deep pothole and snapped the axle.

Luckily, Wardlow Graham had a full assortment of tools in the wagon, so we cut the wagon in half a couple of feet behind the front axle, then wedged the tailgate into place. We fit three oak bows over the bed, forming a frame, over which we draped the canvas.

Sam stepped back and frowned. "Will it work?"

I laughed. "Better'n you think, boy. "Now, move your pony to the tongue, and we'll hook him up."

Hitching the pony to one side of the tongue was awkward, but we made it work. Just after dark, we rolled into camp.

Inside, Margaret informed us that mother and child were doing as well as could be expected.

"Then there's no reason we can't move out in the morning, huh?"

"None at all," Margaret replied. "None at all."

Before sunup the next morning, we pushed east, twenty-five hundred head of goats, two women, two men, a boy, a baby, and a three-legged dog, one of the most unlikely combinations of travelers a man could ever expect to run across.

Margaret drove the wagon at the point of the herd with Shoelink, while Sam flanked and I brought up drag. We could eat dust without it bothering us, but the young mother and her new baby would choke on the fine cloud of white powder thrown up by the herd.

By mid-morning, we had left the rocky canyons behind and moved into a sea of mesquite and cactus spreading over rolling hills. We stopped early for nooning, to give Rebecca and her baby a chance to rest.

Margaret hovered over her and the baby like the proverbial mother hen, much to Rebecca's protests. "You don't have to bother so much with us," she said as Margaret handed her a canteen of water.

"Shush. It's no bother," Margaret replied, her hat hanging on her back, held by the tie cord around her neck. I couldn't help noticing how the sun had browned her skin and lightened streaks in her hair.

Compared to her, Rebecca looked sickly, pale, frail, yet I knew part of that was because she had red hair, and most redheads I'd known were naturally light-complexioned. Still, the worry and fear and pain of the last few days had drained the young woman.

We pulled the wagon up beside an old mesquite. A soft,

warm breeze blew across the countryside, carrying with it the fragrance of spring flowers that lulled us into a state of drowsiness where we lay, sprawled about the small fire.

Naturally, the newborn was the center of attention, everyone wanting to watch him, but he ignored us all, interested only in eating and sleeping.

"Isn't he a beautiful baby?" Margaret watched as Rebecca changed the infant.

I shivered. Somehow the condition the boy had put himself in was not what I called beautiful. "I suppose."

She gave me a puzzled look, then smiled. Her cheeks dimpled. "You men," she muttered, turning away with a shrug.

Sam looked up at me. I arched an eyebrow and shrugged. He snickered.

But to be honest, the baby was no trouble, and Rebecca stood up to the jarring and bouncing with the quiet determination and grit of a seasoned trailhand.

By the end of the second day, I was feeling mighty chipper and pert. Three days to San Antonio, then a week to take Margaret and Sam back to Painted Comanche Tree, and I was off to Wyoming and the Grand Tetons.

We had the Medina and Hondo Rivers to cross, but they would be nothing more than wading ankle-deep water. Beyond them, we had a clear shot into town. And then, I'd put the women and boy up at a nice hotel, dispose of the herd, and find a saloon for a good stiff shot of whiskey.

I rolled into my blankets that night with a whistle on my lips and a dream in my head.

Next thing I knew, a boot was stomping on my lips and kicking at my head.

Chapter Twenty

Stars exploded in my skull. "What the . . ." I rolled away from the sharp toes and tried to jump to my feet, but the blows I'd taken stunned me. I put out my hand, trying to steady myself against the mesquite. A blow knocked my hand away, and I stumbled into the scaly trunk, banging my head and falling to the ground.

Somewhere in the foggy mists filling my brain, I heard shouts and screams. I struggled to reach my feet, but another blow exploded thousands of stars in my head.

And then a long, dizzying fall into black nothingness.

In the distance, garbled voices sounded faintly. Slowly, they drew nearer, and then sudden sensations touched my face. I tried to pull away, but the sensations persisted. A hand lifted the back of my head, and I realized the sensations were water on my face.

"He's waking up." Margaret's voice sounded as if she were speaking from across a large room, hollow and faint.

The first thing I felt was a dull throbbing in my head. Then a sharp pain in my mouth cut through the throbbing, and a warm liquid trickled down my throat.

"Is . . . is he all right?" The distant voice was Sam's.

I struggled to open my eyes. My vision blurred. All I could see were fuzzy outlines silhouetted against the campfire.

159

The hand behind my head lifted me higher. Shoelink came into my vision and stuck some foul-smelling concoction beneath my nose. "*Sangsu* drink. Good for *Sangsu*."

I tried to pull away, but his bony fingers held my head tight. "Drink."

I kept my lips clamped together.

"Gil, you need to drink it." The voice belonged to Margaret. I looked around, trying to focus on her, but like everything else, she was just a blur. "Shoelink says it will take away the soreness. Stop the hurting."

"No." I shook my head. "Schtinks," I mumbled through swollen lips.

Suddenly, fingers seized my nose. I opened my mouth to breathe, and a cup of rank-tasting liquid sloshed down my throat.

I coughed and choked, spitting up some of the gamy liquid. "Ugh. What are you trying to do, kill me?"

Shoelink held my head steady. "*Sangsu* wait. Soon, no hurt. No hurt no more."

Everything around me was coming back into focus, but unfortunately, so were the aches and pains someone had given me. "Who . . . What happened?"

Sam eased a saddle under my head, and Shoelink laid me back gently. "Rustlers, Gil," Sam answered. "Five of them. They sneaked up on us and stole the herd after they knocked you out." His words ran together like a litter of puppies fighting over a steak bone.

"Rustlers?" I explored the inside of my mouth with my tongue, where I discovered several loose teeth, the source of the warm blood running down my throat.

Margaret took up the story. "They were the ones who tried it once before. The one who beat you up said to tell you it was payback time."

I paused in testing my teeth. "Payback?"

"For the bullet in the shoulder."

"Oh." I remembered the jasper I'd knocked out of the saddle back in the canyon, when they were dodging the swinging boulders. I tried to grin. "I'd say from the way I feel that he probably got the best of the deal." I winced and spat out a tooth.

Rebecca looked on, her infant clutched to her breast, her eyes wide with fear. Margaret chuckled at me. "You're not the prettiest sight right now."

My vision blurred. I blinked. It remained blurred, and I realized that my eyes were swelling shut.

Shoelink put his hands over my eyes. "*Sangsu* close eyes. Zhou Gui Ling make better."

The fetid concoction he had poured down my throat had relaxed me, and slowly, the aches and pains began to fade. He laid a damp rag over my eyes. I grimaced at the stinging sensation, and then I must have fallen asleep, for the next thing I remember, the sun was high over head when I opened my eyes.

I lay still, afraid to move.

But, to my surprise, I felt like I would live. My face looked like a litter of hogs had rooted it up, but to my bewilderment, I didn't hurt—too bad. And I could see.

I felt my eyes. There was no swelling. I looked at Shoelink. "How did you do that?"

He dipped his head. "Honorable grandfather. He much wise. He show . . . us . . . his childen secrets to make us . . . better."

"You could almost see the swelling going down," Margaret said. "It was unbelievable. Every time we looked, more of the swelling had gone away."

With a groan, I managed to scoot up into a sitting position. Slowly, the cobwebs in my head disappeared, and I began to link one thought to the next in some semblance of logic.

A cup of coffee appeared in my hand. Eagerly, I sipped it, wincing as the liquid burned the cuts inside my mouth. "They get the whole herd?" I looked up at Margaret.

"Yes. And the horses."

For a moment, her words failed to register. "The horses?"

Sam spoke up. "Yeah, Gil. They took the horses. We're on foot. Again."

Suddenly, the coffee went cold in my hands. I glanced at Rebecca, who was sitting with her back to us, nursing her child. I looked up at Margaret, and in her eyes saw the same concern I had about the baby.

"What about rifles?" I looked about the camp.

"They took them all," Margaret replied, her face showing the strain of the last thirty-six hours. "Your handgun too," she said as I reached for my side arm.

My hand froze in midair. A rush of red-hot anger surged through my veins, filling me with a deadly determination.

"Da . . ." Sam tore loose with a curse, but he cut it off in midword when I cut my eyes at him. His cheeks colored and he gave Margaret a sidelong glance. "I mean, dadgum."

Shoelink spoke up. "Missy not right. Rustlers leave one."

"What?"

He nodded and disappeared behind a mesquite and returned with a Winchester. He wore that silly grin.

I chuckled. "They leave it, or did you put it there?"

He shrugged. "We need, yes?"

"Yes." I eyed the Winchester gratefully. "We need it bad if we're going to get out of here."

Margaret crossed her legs and squatted beside me. ''What are we going to do?''

Everyone was staring at me, expecting some kind of miracle. But I didn't have any miracles, except plain old hardheaded stubbornness. ''Well, I could catch up with them like last time, but they'll be expecting it. I figure the best thing we can do is start walking. To San Antone.''

''Walking?'' Margaret glanced over her shoulder to the east. ''How far is it?''

I ran my fingers through my hair. ''Not far. Forty miles or so.'' I eyed Rebecca and the child. ''We'll take it easy. Five or six days, we'll be there.''

Rebecca tightened her grip about her child, pressing the small boy to her breast. Her eyes registered fear for her and the baby.

I tried to ease her concern. ''We'll travel slow and easy, Mrs. Graham. We'll take turns carrying the baby so as not to wear you out.''

She started to protest, but I gave her a lopsided grin and explained. ''We can't afford for the mother to get too tired. After all, she's the one who takes care of the boy at night while the rest of us are sleeping.''

Rebecca smiled. A tear glistened in the corner of her eye.

''One thing, though. If we catch the herd, I plan to swing around it and be waiting for them in San Antone. With only one rifle, we don't have a chance.'' I lumbered to my feet and added in a gruff voice, ''Let's pack up and move out.''

We didn't have much gear to move out. All the rustlers left us were our soogans, canteens, cooking utensils, a parfleche of flour, and enough coffee for two, maybe three pots.

* * *

The day was hot and steamy. We rested half a dozen times in the patchy shade of mesquites before camping at sundown. Shoelink pulled another miracle by adding a strange mixture of spices to a ball of dough and frying up some right tasty tortillas, wrapped around juicy white meat.

Margaret and Sam licked their lips. "Wow, this is sure good," the boy muttered, reaching for another.

Rebecca nibbled. "This is delicious, Mr. Shoelink. What is it?"

The diminutive Oriental stared at her thoughtfully. He stammered for the right word, then said something that sounded like *"yung, yung."*

I don't know if that was the Chinese word or not, and I don't know if he was telling the truth or not, but I wasn't about to let her know we were eating rattlesnake. A white lie was in order. *"Yung, yung* is Chinese for rabbit, Mrs. Graham." I added hastily, "And you're mighty right. This rabbit is real tasty."

Margaret frowned. "Rabbit? But, there's no bones."

I lied again. "Yeah. Yeah. Shoelink cut them out before broiling it."

She looked at me, then at Shoelink, who nodded emphatically. With a shrug, Margaret turned back to her Chinese rabbit.

Before I turned in that night, Shoelink handed me a cup of liquid. I smelled it and deferred the drink, but he insisted. "Much good . . . *Sangsu.* Make good." He pounded his chest. "Make okay."

Despite my reluctance, I drank the concoction. I cringed. I trembled. And then I gagged. The drink tasted like liquid skunk.

The next evening, we dined on Chinese rabbit again, and again everyone licked their fingers and asked for seconds.

Shoelink just gave me one of his inscrutable grins and turned back to the tortillas. I ate gingerly, for my loosened teeth had not yet tightened, and every move of my jaw broke loose some of the scabs forming over the cuts and bruises the rustlers had dealt me.

And naturally, Shoelink showed up with my bedtime toddy, liquid skunk.

The next three days were like the first two, one foot in front of the other, break for rest in the shade, then we'd heave ourselves to our feet and try for another few miles. Our feet hurt, but we grew tougher. Each torturous step I took hammered another nail in my resolve and determination. When I faced those yahoos, I would do it with the cool confidence that comes from knowing nothing can stop you.

And each day, Shoelink came up with new and different ways to prepare *yung, yung*. We ate it baked, broiled, burned, roasted, stewed, fried, and fricasseed.

Mrs. Graham ate for two, her and the baby. And Margaret was no slouch. She looked up at Shoelink once and remarked, ''One thing that puzzles me. How do you catch these rabbits? You don't shoot them.''

The diminutive Chinese just stared at her, frowning, his head cocked to the side. I eyed the small man with a growing suspicion that Shoelink understood only what he wanted to understand, and if he didn't want to answer or explain, he simply—frowned.

''How does he do it, Gil?''

Margaret's redirected question caught me by surprise. I thought fast, not one of my long suits. I'd been lying about the rattlesnake all along, so I figured I might as well keep lying. ''Traps. Yeah. He traps them. That's what he does, he traps them.''

Sam exclaimed, ''Wow. Will you teach me how to trap rabbits, Mr. Shoelink? Huh? Will you, huh?''

Shoelink just frowned at the boy.

Sam looked at me. ''Will he, Gil, huh? Will he?''

I eyed Shoelink murderously. ''You bet he will, boy. You bet he will.''

The sixth night, we camped on a hill that rose above the others. Below us was the Medina River, and in the distance, on the horizon, lights blinked. Rebecca Graham cradled her baby and stared through the darkness. ''Is that San Antonio?''

I nodded, my own eyes fixed on the lights. My aches and pains had disappeared, thanks to the rugged travel and the rancorous concoction Shoelink prepared for me each night.

''You suppose those rustlers already got the herd there?'' asked Sam.

''I reckon. We didn't run across them. All they had to do was make a few miles a day. Probably had no trouble doing that.''

Sam's forehead wrinkled as he stared expectantly at me. I could feel Margaret's eyes on the back of my head. I knew the question on their minds, but I didn't volunteer the answer. The answer was the only answer that me or any jasper could give, the only answer that any Westerner could give, and they both knew it without having to ask.

Margaret spoke in a low voice. ''You're going after them when we hit town, aren't you?''

Rebecca gasped and spun to face me, her eyes wide.

''Reckon so. But I'll go to the law first,'' I replied, squatting and nonchalantly pouring the last of my coffee on the fire.

"What if the law don't do nothing?" Sam looked up at me earnestly.

"Then, I reckon it's up to me."

"But, there was five or six of them, Gil," said Sam. "That's too many."

I glanced up at Rebecca, then fixed my eyes on Sam. "They stole from us, boy. They took our horses and left us for dead. There's no choice. They do it to us and get away with it, maybe they'll bury the next ones they steal from. Back in the East, there's law, but here, we have to give it a kick in the seat of the pants sometimes. That's all I'm doing, helping it along." I studied him a moment, then added, "This is the West, boy. If you can't handle it, maybe you oughta think about returning to the East."

For several seconds, no one spoke, then Margaret laid her hand on my arm. "Do what you have to do. Don't worry about us."

She had a brave, trembling smile on her face. I wondered if that was how my own mother must have looked when she gave up all she owned back in Tennessee and moved to Texas with my pa. Men might have made Texas, but it was the women who made the men.

Shoelink remained seated, staring at the fire. Reading his feelings was like trying to outbluff a Mississippi riverboat gambler.

Chapter Twenty-one

A soft wind blew through the mesquite, and the leaves danced like skittish shadows in the glow cast by the dying fire. I studied every frolicking leaf above my head. I couldn't sleep. I had no idea what I was facing the next day. All I knew was that I had to take back what had been stolen from us, from Sam, from Shoelink, from me. And while I was doing that, I could pay back some of the fear and terror they had caused Rebecca and Margaret.

The stars seemed brighter than I had ever seen them that night, the air sweeter, the laughter happier. Maybe there was something about a man on his way to the hanging tree suddenly realizing just how much he had, how rich he really was. I don't know about that jasper, but while I lay there and watched the Big Dipper rotate around the North Star, Sam's ranch back in the Franklin Mountains seemed like my own Garden of Eden. If I could have been back there, I would have been happy to deal with the serpent and his apple.

Around four, I rose and fed kindling to the banked fire, after which I put on the coffee, leery of the taste, for this was the third time we'd used the grounds.

"You're up early." Margaret's voice broke through the crackle of kindling catching fire.

I grinned over my shoulder at her. "I'm a morning person."

168

She sat up. Despite her disheveled hair, despite the wrinkles in her dimpled cheek from lying in one position too long, she was prettier than a field of Texas bluebonnets. ''Me too.''

When I didn't reply, she continued. ''Pa always took his coffee out on the porch and watched the sun come up. I got in the habit with him when I was just a child, and I've been doing it ever since.''

For a moment, I relaxed, pushing the upcoming showdown from my mind. I squinted through the mesquite at the graying horizon. Lights were beginning to flicker on in San Antonio. ''Good habit. Makes a jasper realize that every day is a fresh start, that he can make a new beginning.''

Margaret dragged her comb through her short hair, yanking out some tangles. She tried to appear nonchalant, but the tiny tremors in her voice gave her away. ''I don't know if you've ever noticed, but Pa built our house so it faced the rising sun. He built enough windows so the sun would fill the house no matter what time of year. Why, he even wanted to add a room and make it completely out of glass, but Ma put her foot down. Can't you imagine what would have happened if one of our famous hailstorms came along? Why, Ma, she. . . .''

I chuckled to myself. She was beginning to babble, so I interrupted her. ''Your pa is a good man. He built a fine ranch. A fine ranch.''

She paused in combing her hair, then laid the comb in her lap. She swallowed hard. ''What do you figure will happen when you find them?''

''I don't know.'' I poured us a cup of coffee and took a tentative sip. I shivered. Coffee wasn't made to be used over, not three times. Still, if you don't have something, you make do with what's available.

Margaret cringed at the coffee, but she drank it dutifully. It was hot, and it had a flavor, though the taste reminded me more of a pair of socks at the end of a trail drive.

Slowly, the camp roused, and before the sun rose, we were on the trail. At noon, we struck the road to Piedras Negras. San Antonio was only three miles ahead.

San Antonio was a busy, bustling village of adobe and stick jacales sprawled along the San Antonio River. Despite our travel-worn appearance, we attracted no attention as we wound along the village streets to a small hotel just a short distance from the Alamo.

"After we all get settled in our rooms, I'll nose about town and see what I can find out about the herd. I don't reckon too many goat herds come through here, so they shouldn't be hard to locate."

Sam looked around the room I had secured for the three of us. "I want to go with you. I don't want to stay here."

I shook my head. "Nope. And no argument. You stay here with Shoelink." I turned to the little Chinese. "You hear? Keep the boy with you."

Shoelink dipped his head. "Ai. What *Sangsu* say, Zhou Gui Ling do."

I felt fit. I had healed quickly. No germ in existence could have survived a forty-mile hike in the blazing Texas sun on top of a daily bath in that appalling concoction Shoelink poured down me every night.

Still, butterflies tumbled about in my stomach. I was never any shakes as a fighter. Couldn't really see the sense in it or what it gained an hombre, but then there were times a man had no choice, when he had to fight. When that time came, he was a walleyed fool if he held back and didn't put every ounce of his effort into the task.

I found me a Colt .44 at a local gun shop. Up in my room, I sat on the bed and dismantled the handgun, taking care to clean it well. With Sam and Shoelink looking on, I did the same with the Winchester. Where I was going, I didn't want a grain of sand or a fragment of a twig to get in the way. My last step was to fill the cartridge loops on my gun belt with hundred-and-eighty-five-grain slugs.

Shoelink and Sam watched silently.

I drew a deep breath and looked at Sam and Shoelink. "I'll be back directly. I'll go to the law first. Maybe that's all we'll need to do."

The worry in Sam's eyes vanished. "You mean, you can get the herd back without a fight?"

I didn't look at Shoelink. The little Oriental could read every thought in my head. "Sure. Nothing to worry about. Now, you do like I said. You stay here with Shoelink, okay?"

Sam nodded eagerly. "Sure, Gil. Don't worry. I won't get out of his sight."

The sun had set, pulling the dark blanket of night over the village. The air was warm, perfumed with the sweetness of honeysuckle and gardenias, sharp with fried onions and barbecued *cabra*, tangy from the gallons of wine and barrels of beer in every open-door saloon along the street, and filled with laughter and merriment from bands of roving dancers.

Outside the first saloon, I tugged my hat down over my eyes. I stepped inside and casually made my way around the crowded tables to the bar. "Whiskey."

The Mexican bartender eyed me suspiciously until I plopped down a half eagle. He poured a drink and left the bottle on the bar. I quickly downed the drink, shivered at the raw liquid, and poured another. I leaned my elbows on the bar and stared down at my drink, my ears tuned to the myriad conversations behind me.

After a few minutes, I turned and leaned against the bar, whiskey in hand, and studied the crowd. Mostly Mexican, with a few gringos mixed about. I didn't know exactly what I was looking for. I just figured I'd recognize it when I saw it.

No one paid me any attention. After downing my second raw drink, I meandered outside and joined in with the aimlessly wandering vaqueros and cowboys on the streets. After two more saloons with an equal amount of no success, I decided to find the stockyards. Find out for sure if the goats were here.

The stockyards were easy to find. Just follow your nose.

Sure enough, one pen was full of goats. I couldn't tell if they were ours or not. I didn't have enough goat sense to recognize one from the other. To me, a goat was a goat, and I didn't spend a whole lot of time studying them. As far as I knew, the three or four cowpokes hanging around the stockyard might be the rustlers. I didn't want them to get suspicious, so I moved on.

Next to the goat pen was a corral of beeves. I leaned up against the top rail and studied the cows. One hombre sidled around to me. "Interested in some stock, cowboy?"

I glanced at him. He wore a suit and vest, and he was too clean and too fat to be a line-riding cowpoke. "Might be. These yours?"

"On consignment." He offered me his hand. "Name's J. C. Peake." He made a sweeping gesture with his arm. "Cattle broker. This here's my place. I buy and sell, and only the best stock. You never get no culls from J. C. Peake," he added.

I had the feeling he had used those words more than once. In fact, he struck me as the shyster type who'd insist those sentiments or something similar be engraved on his headstone: J. C. PEAKE. HE NEVER HANDED OUT CULLS.

"Cattle, huh?" I nodded to the goats. "That don't look like cattle to me."

J. C. laughed robustly. "No, they don't, friend. Special buy. Company up north is screaming for goats. I pay three dollars a head, then ship them to St. Louis. I don't know where they go from there, but from what I hear, the market will stay lively for goats another three, maybe four years."

"Not bad." I played dumb. "You getting ready to send those goats north?"

"Yep. Bought twenty-five hundred yesterday. Finished out a trainload."

I acted impressed. "Twenty-five hundred. That's a heap of greenbacks."

"Yep."

"This hombre you bought them from, reckon he's looking for hands to bring in more goats or something? I could use a job."

J. C. shrugged and pulled a cigar from his vest pocket. "Don't know. He had four or five hands with him. Might have a full crew."

I laughed. "That'd be my luck, but I think I'll ask anyway. Worst he can say is no."

J. C. joined in the laughter, his rotund belly shaking. "Reckon you're right, cowboy." He grew serious. "You in a hurry to get out of San Antone?"

"Just traveling through. Why?"

"Well, I'm thinking about expanding, and you seem like the kind of jasper that can let a bad answer roll off. That's a good quality in the selling business."

I shrugged. "Don't know. I'm just a cowpoke. Reckon I'd be like a rattlesnake on a hot rock in your kind of business."

He laughed again. "Well, think it over. The old boy who sold me the goats is down at the Menger Hotel. Name's Latimer, Burl Latimer."

"Thanks. And I'll keep your offer in mind, Mr. Peake. Who knows? I might be a better salesman than I think."

I was no salesman, but as I stomped down the dusty street toward the Menger, I figured that when I finished with Burl Latimer, he would be one hombre more than willing to buy the notion that he made one big mistake when he stole our herd and kicked me around.

Chapter Twenty-two

The Menger was a fancy hotel by my standards. On one side of the large, airy lobby, a flight of stairs led to the second floor, while on the adjoining wall, an archway opened into a crowded dining room.

Winchester in hand, I sauntered up to the check-in counter and asked for Burl Latimer. "I heard he was hiring."

The clerk shrugged. "Don't know about that, mister, but that's him in yonder." He nodded to half a dozen hardcases sitting around a table just inside the dining room doors. "The one with the beard is Mr. Latimer. You got here just in time. He checked out ten minutes ago and went in there for a last drink before he and his boys hit the trail."

From where I stood, Latimer looked mighty rugged, and the owlhoots surrounding him appeared just as tough. Six to one wasn't my kind of odds, but Old Man Time had just taken a hand in the game, and if I didn't act fast, Latimer and his boys would skedaddle from San Antonio.

I jerked to a halt. Latimer rose and spoke to his boys, patted his lean belly, then headed for the front door. I grinned at my luck. I could get him outside, all by his lonesome.

He was a large man, taller than me and about twenty pounds heavier. He pushed through the stained glass doors and paused on the porch to light a cigar. He drew deeply and blew a stream of smoke into the night air.

That's when I jabbed my .44 in his back. "Easy, Latimer. Don't make any sudden moves or I'll put a hole in your carcass to drive a wagon through."

The large man froze, then relaxed. "Joe, I told you I'd stomp you to a puddle next time you pulled this kind of stunt on me."

I jabbed the muzzle harder, and this time I felt it hit a belt, a padded belt. I had to grin. This was too easy. "This ain't Joe, and I'm dead honest about that hole. Now around the corner."

Latimer did as he was told. "Listen, friend. I got no money if that's what you're after. I just got into town and was looking for a grubstake."

The shadows along the side of the Menger were broken by shafts of yellow light spilling from the windows. "Hold it right there, Latimer." I stopped him in the middle of a pool of light while I remained in the shadows.

"Okay, hombre. Just don't get itchy."

"Now, turn around."

The bearded outlaw turned and squinted into the darkness, but he couldn't make me out.

"All right. You got me. What's your pleasure?"

"Seventy-five hundred dollars, mister. That's my pleasure."

He started to open his mouth to protest, but I cut him off. "Don't lie. You got it on you, in that belt under your shirt."

His face grew hard. "You think I'm going to let a thief take . . ."

I cocked the hammer, and he clamped his mouth shut. "Shut up. You're the thief, Latimer. That was my herd you stole and sold to J. C. Peake. That's my seventy-five hun-

dred in that belt around your belly. There's no way you and John Howard are going to steal our money and get away with it. Now, you be a good boy and hand it over.''

Latimer snorted. ''John Howard. Ha. That gutless old man. He don't have nothing I want. And I don't have nothing he can have.''

The owlhoot's admission surprised me, but the anger boiling my blood kept my finger tight on the trigger. ''I'm not saying it again. Give me that belt.''

He glared at me. ''If I don't?''

I sighed. ''Son, it ain't going to bother me to take it from your cold carcass. It would just be a heap sight easier for both of us if you did what I said. But when you really get down to it, it don't make a whole lot of difference to me.'' My voice grew cold and icy. ''Now, you can shuck that belt, or I'll do it for you.''

Reluctantly, he unbuttoned his shirt and unfastened the belt. He was desperate. Despite the shadows, I could see the glint in his eyes. I knew what he had in mind, and I prepared myself for it, but the large outlaw moved faster than I expected.

He whipped the belt out and slapped the six-gun from my hand. With a roar, he lunged at me.

I ducked my head and rammed my shoulder into his belly, lifting his feet from the ground and driving him back against the side of the Menger.

He grunted, then brought both his fists down on my back, trying to drive me to the ground. ''You dirty . . .''

I stopped the spewing of guttural words by bringing my head up against the point of his chin. ''Try that on for size.''

Stepping back, I slammed my fists into his hard stomach. It was like hitting the side of a locomotive.

Out of nowhere, a blow struck my ear. My head exploded, and for a moment, I felt like I was falling. I reached out and grabbed Latimer, pulling him with me.

We hit the ground rolling, poking, biting, and kicking. There was no science in the fight, no backing away for the other hombre to climb to his feet, no fancy dancing and jabbing and bobbing and weaving, but a brawling, scrapping, no-holds-barred effort to batter the other man to a pulp.

I jerked my head back in pain as Latimer jabbed his thumb into my eye. A fist caught me in the side of the neck, almost paralyzing me. I staggered to my feet and swung a looping right that touched nothing but the air.

The larger man grabbed my neck and tried to strangle me. I clenched my teeth and swung at his heart, slamming fist after fist into his breast and ribs. My head grew light, but I kept punching, one crushing blow after the other.

Abruptly, his hands fell away, and he stumbled from the patch of light into the darkness. I leaped at the burly outlaw, my lips bleeding, my vision blurred.

In the darkness, we could not see each other, but we continued to swing, sometimes connecting, sometimes missing. A set of bony knuckles bounced off my forehead and another almost tore my shoulder from my torso. He gave an ugly laugh.

Incensed, I threw a wild punch. My fist caught his chin, and he grunted. Just as I swung again and missed, I heard Latimer bang against the side of the hotel, a result of the blow to his chin. I lumbered forward, my head down, swinging sharp, vicious left and right hooks. The first couple blistered air, but then I reached him and battered his ribs.

All of a sudden, he wrapped his huge arms around me, pinning my arms to my side and lifting me in a crushing bear hug. I twisted and squirmed, but he held me tight.

Without warning, I popped my head forward and slammed my forehead against his nose.

"Why you. . . ." He cursed and dropped me.

As soon as my feet hit the ground, I charged, slamming him back against the wall and putting every ounce of strength I had left into an uppercut.

I winced as my knuckles caught the point of his chin. A explosion of air whooshed from his lungs, and the burly outlaw sagged forward, throwing his arms over my shoulders in one last futile effort. I stepped back, and he hit the ground at my feet, right beside the money belt, in the middle of the patch of light from the window.

I stood motionless, my head thrown back, sucking great draughts of air into my burning lungs. In front of the hotel, the door slammed and voices drifted into the alley. Quickly, I grabbed the money belt with the seventy-five hundred dollars and turned to leave.

"Well, well. Look what we got here." Three of Latimer's boys stood at the edge of the light.

"Yeah. We got us a thief, boys," came a voice from behind me.

I spun. A fist shot out of the darkness and busted me right between the eyes. I sprawled backward in the dirt, the belt clenched in my fingers like death. I grabbed for my six-gun, but a boot heel stomped my wrist.

"That ain't nice, cowpoke," one of the outlaws growled.

"No, it ain't," said another as the five gathered over me.

"Looks like he took old Burl apart," said another.

"Yeah," answered a fourth. "I told Burl he shoulda let us take care of the whole bunch back in the canyon instead of just shooting over their heads."

"Reckon that'll teach Burl to not be so easy."

Another guffawed. "Makes no difference now. We'll

just kick this old boy's head in now. That'll make up for it.''

I bunched my muscles, ready to leap to my feet. I wasn't taking a beating lying down.

''Aiiiiyeee.'' A shrill shout ripped the darkness apart, and one outlaw's head snapped back as a pair of feet slammed into his back, hurling him into the owlhoot at his side.

A bedlam of wild shouts echoed through the alley. Two more outlaws groaned and crumpled to the ground. Sam and Margaret stepped into the light, each waving an ax handle and wearing a ferocious grin.

The fifth outlaw grabbed for his six-gun, but Margaret swung the white oak ax handle and broke his knee. He shouted and fell to the ground just before Sam coldcocked his man with an ax handle between the eyes.

I struggled to sit up. I couldn't believe my eyes. Ten seconds earlier, I was ready for a beating, and now my tormentors were sprawled unconscious around me. Shoelink stepped into the light and dipped his head to me.

Sam grinned. ''We figured you might need some help.''

I tried to laugh, but my face hurt. ''You're sure a welcome sight. Here, help me up.''

We paused over Burl Latimer. He was slowly coming around. ''Latimer, you and your scum get out of San Antone. I see you tomorrow, I'm going to the law.''

He glared at me.

''Let's go,'' I said, and, leaning on Margaret and Sam, I made my way back to the hotel. I hurt with every step, but I had never been more proud of anyone than I was of those three.

I grinned down at Margaret. ''You handled yourself pretty good back there.''

She arched an eyebrow. "Let that be a lesson. I can be tough."

"Yes, Ma'am." I squeezed Sam's shoulder. "I certainly do believe that."

Sam laughed.

I glanced at Shoelink. "Never thought I'd say this, but I reckon I need a dose of your liquid skunk tonight."

Shoelink nodded. "Ai. I make."

The next morning, a banging at the door awakened me.

Burl Latimer and the sheriff stood glaring at me. "That's him, Sheriff. That's the thief. He's got my seventy-five hundred dollars that my boys and me made selling our herd of goats to J. C. Peake."

The commotion awakened Margaret and Rebecca across the hall.

"He's lying, Sheriff," Margaret exclaimed. "They stole the herd from us back at the Frio River."

"She's crazy, Sheriff," Latimer replied. "Like a loon."

The sheriff scratched his jaw. "What do you have to say, mister?"

"Look, Sheriff. The herd belongs to this boy here." I quickly explained the situation. "Then, like the lady said, five days back, this owlhoot and his cohorts stole everything. We had to walk in, and the lady over there with a brand-new baby."

"A baby, you say?" The sheriff looked around, and Rebecca nodded.

"Hate to hear a story like that," he replied, turning back to me, "but it's your word against his. You got any proof the herd's the boy's?"

My temper flared, but I kept it under control. "Does he have any proof it's his?" I nodded to Latimer, whose face was bruised and battered, almost as bad as mine.

The sheriff mulled the question. "Good point. How do we prove who owned the herd?"

Shoelink pushed forward. "Excuse, please."

Latimer made a move to push the diminutive Oriental away, but Shoelink's hands were a blur, and Latimer found himself with an arm twisted up behind his back. "Ow. Hey."

"Excuse, please," said Shoelink, dropping the arm and stepping back. "I show sheriff answer he asks. Come."

The sheriff looked at me. I gestured for him to follow Shoelink. I grabbed my six-gun, jumped into my boots, and followed.

We were a strange entourage stomping down the street, half a dozen skimpily dressed people tagging after a small Chinese man who was pitter-pattering down the street in short, choppy steps.

Just outside the corral, Shoelink stopped. He motioned to the gate. "Please, *Sangsu*. The gate."

Frowning, I did as he said.

With the gate open, Shoelink began singing his trail song, that tiny, lilting jumble of words I never could understand. He turned and pitter-pattered up the dusty street.

"Hey, what the blazes you think you're doing?" shouted Latimer. "You're turning them goats loose."

Shoelink ignored him. He continued singing, and one by one, the goats left the corral and fell into line behind the diminutive Oriental.

Latimer's face grew red as he realized what was happening before his eyes.

Shoelink led the goats up the street, down the alley on one side of the Menger, and up the alley on the other side of the hotel, and then back to the corral, singing his lyrical song. And the goats followed one by one, until they had all returned to the corral.

I closed the gate and turned to the sheriff. "Well?"

The sheriff glared at Latimer. "Mister, you have five minutes to get out of town. After that, you're going to jail for cattle steal . . . I mean, goat stealing."

Latimer was livid with rage. He sputtered at me. "You. I'll get you. Just you wait and see. I'll . . ."

Something in me snapped. I was tired of threats. I was tired of Sam and Margaret and all of us being mistreated. From now on, no one was going to hurt any of us.

I eased aside and flipped the rawhide loop from my six-gun. "Shut up, Latimer. I've got a bellyful of your whining. I'm calling you out. Pony up to your big talk or crawl out of here on your belly." I leaned forward, my fingers outstretched over the butt of my .44.

His eyes blazed, then widened in surprise. He tried to bluster his way out of it. "Not here. Not now."

I pushed the showdown. "Yeah. Here. Now." I stepped forward and slapped him across the face. I struggled to hold my temper. "Unless you're a coward."

"Why, you . . ."

I slapped him again, backing him up. "You're a coward, Latimer. A four-flushing coward."

By now, a crowd had gathered on the boardwalks.

"And everyone out here can see what a coward you are." I slapped him again. Blood dribbled down the edges of his lips.

His eyes grew wild. He glanced about, but I wouldn't let him run. "You're going to fight me, Latimer, and when you do, I'll plant you six feet under." I slapped him again. His nose started to bleed. "Draw. You hear me, you stinking coward? Draw!"

His hand trembled over the butt of his six-gun. Seconds passed, long seconds. Fear filled his eyes, and his shoulders sagged.

In disgust, I grabbed his six-gun and threw it in the water trough. "Get out of here. Next time I see you, you're a dead man."

"You think he'll be back, Gil?" Margaret looked across the table at me.

"I doubt it."

"You shamed him."

"I saved his life." I paused and tried to explain it to Sam. "Latimer's kind is everywhere, boy. Bullies. But when a man stands up to them, they crumble. They always have, and they always will. That's why you can't ever let anyone run over you. Make sure you're right, then stand up for yourself."

Margaret smiled. "Just be sure you're right, Sam. Be sure."

"Yeah. Be real sure." I hesitated, then said to Margaret, "I was wrong about John Howard. I confronted Latimer, but he bragged that he wouldn't have nothing to do with the man. Called Howard a gutless old man."

She arched an eyebrow. Instead of "I told you so," she replied, "Anyone would have figured like you did. In fact, I was beginning to wonder."

I grinned at her. "Thanks."

Rebecca entered the room with her baby. She sat at the table and smiled. "I've decided on a name for the boy."

We looked at her expectantly. She stared at me wistfully. "I'm going to name him Gilbert Joseph Graham. Joseph after my husband, and Gilbert after you, Gil."

My throat burned, and for the first time in seventeen years, I fought back tears. "Well, Mrs. Graham, that's right nice of you, but Gilbert is a mighty cumbersome handle to stick on a younker."

She eyed me levelly. "It's the name of a man, a real man. And I'm proud for my son to bear it."

I looked at Margaret. She glowed, like one of those roses in Wild Rose Pass. Sam grinned like a lovesick hound, and Shoelink stared at me with a twinkle in his eyes. I suddenly realized just how rich I was, how important I was to those around me. I suddenly realized I had found a home.

"What are your plans now, Mrs. Graham?"

She glanced at Margaret and then smiled sadly. "Well, I left word for Joseph. Margaret invited me back to the Franklin Mountains, to Wild Rose Pass. Little Gil and me don't have family or friends anywhere except here with you all. I can't think of a better place to be." She paused, and a look of pain filled her eyes. "If Joseph is alive, he'll hear where I am. He'll come."

I studied Margaret. She met my gaze, and a warm smile dimpled her rosy cheeks. I glanced to the north, toward the Tetons. I cleared my throat. "Well, boy, I reckon we'd better get busy. We've got a bit of shopping to do before we start back." I winked at Sam. "Running a ranch takes a heap of equipment and supplies, and we sure don't want to run short."

Margaret's smile grew wider.

Sam looked at me in surprise. "You mean . . . what about Wyoming? The Tetons?"

I looked at Margaret when I answered the boy's question. "I tell you, son. Wyoming's got nothing to compare with what I've got right here. Besides, I figure there's enough room left on Painted Comanche Tree to add our own history."

Sam whooped.

Rebecca cried.

And for the first time, Shoelink laughed aloud.